THE LION'S TALE

Akhil K. writes in Malayalam. He lives in Kannur and currently works as a daily-wage JCB operator by day. He had to discontinue his education after school in order to support his family, working as a newspaper delivery boy in the mornings and at a sand mine by night.

His novels include *Simhathinte Katha*, *Tharakanthan* and *Muthappan*. *Neelachadayan*, his first short story collection, won the 2022 Geetha Hiranyan Endowment Award from the Kerala Sahitya Akademi. He has also received the Youth Icon Award instituted by the Kerala State Youth Commission and the Indian Writers Forum's O.V. Vijayan Memorial Award.

Sarita Ravindranath is a writer and editor based in Chennai.

THE LION'S TALE

AKHIL K.

TRANSLATED BY
SARITA RAVINDRANATH

ekadā

ekadā

First published in Malayalam as *Simhathinte Katha* in 2022 by Mathrubhumi Books

Published in English as *The Lion's Tale* in 2025 by Ekadā, an imprint of Westland Books, a division of Nasadiya Technologies Private Limited

No. 269/2B, First Floor, 'Irai Arul', Vimalraj Street, Nethaji Nagar, Alapakkam Main Road, Maduravoyal, Chennai 600095

Westland, the Westland logo, Ekadā and the Ekadā logo are the trademarks of Nasadiya Technologies Private Limited, or its affiliates.

ISBN: 9789371977081

10 9 8 7 6 5 4 3 2 1

This is a work of fiction. Names, characters, organisations, places, events and incidents are either products of the author's imagination or used fictitiously.

Typeset by Jojy Philip

Printed at Parksons Graphics Pvt. Ltd

Contents

The Call of Ekarmala

That night, the sky laid out a dazzling array of stars with the finesse of a salesman. It was the night when Saravanan and Aadi decided to work for a living.

The job? Dress up as a ghost; wait by the narrow dirt roads spread across the valleys of Ekarmala at night; rush towards any lone, unsuspecting pedestrian and scare them away.

At first, Saravanan laughed and felt a tinge of pity when Aadi narrated the plan. You would have to be absurdly naive to think that people would be afraid of ghostly apparitions in this day and age.

But Aadi turned out to be right. 'It takes very little to frighten people. Fear is like a beast curled up within the soul. Snap your fingers and it rises to the surface, consuming everything else.'

Within six weeks, fear spread like an epidemic across the countryside.

It all began when a man who worked with the local hooch distillers approached Saravanan. Saravanan did not know his name then: Rajan. A man with a physique so lean that it seemed poverty had taken up residence within his slight frame. Even though Saravanan had run into Rajan many times, he had never felt the need to smile or exchange pleasantries.

But on a star-spangled night, Rajan came looking for Saravanan and Aadi. Until Aadi said yes to Rajan, Saravanan had never imagined in his wildest dreams that they would ever work for money.

When Saravanan and Rajan met Aadi, he was lying on his back, on a mound of earth in the saline fields, staring at the sky. Aadi liked these mounds, heaped piles of mud and mulch created when farmers planted coconut trees in the marshy soil of his village. When the trees died, the elevated structures would lose their purpose. Aadi would often sit on these mounds, as if on a throne. The mounds, he would imagine, served as memorials to dead trees. Whenever Saravanan saw Aadi in his seat, dark memories would rush in.

'You know all about us, Aadi,' said Rajan. 'Everyone here knows that we transport both women and hooch across the hill. But the boys now feel a need for secrecy. No one should come up the hill, poking their noses into our business. Do what you must, but once it turns dark, people should be afraid to even cast a fleeting glance at Ekarmala. We can give you the cash and henchmen. Just tell us what else you need.'

Rajan, resembling a friendly chieftain, stood below the mound and looked up at Aadi. Aadi's piercing laugh rang through the night air. He got down from his perch and raised a fist at Rajan. 'Who told you that Chindachchan's son is the right person for this job?' His tone was ominous.

Rajan seemed to get a measure of Aadi's anger as he replied softly, 'No one. I see Saravanan and you hanging around here sleeplessly at night. If I give the job to someone else, they'll have to get rid of you two first. I thought it was better to ask you instead.'

Aadi didn't quite know how to respond to that logic. He stood still, speechless, feeling as pointless as a headless coconut tree.

Nature runs wild in most parts around Ekarmala. Humans occupy only one part of the hill, living in eight hamlets along the Vannathi river. A bridge, built by laying coconut trunks and sand across the river, connects the villages to the mainland. There are swamps all around. Acres of marshland, inundated fields and empty mounds of earth. On the edges of one side of the mainland is a dense forest called Peelimudi, and round the other edge flows the Vannathi. Ekarmala stands trapped in the middle, a proud animal that holds its head high despite being pinned down from all sides.

'Do you truly believe we can scare people away by dressing up as ghosts?' Saravanan raised a doubt as he painted Aadi's face with a mix of red and black pigments, followed by bold white strokes across the cheeks.

'Why so sceptical? Fear is always present within us. Fear is the mind's primal form. The human brain developed from exposure to light and a sense of community. Take away the bright lights and the comfort of crowds, and a man gets restless. Stoke the fear a little when a man is alone in the dark, and he stands no chance,' Aadi said confidently.

Saravanan handed him a mirror, and Aadi gazed at his reflection.

Saravanan could hear his heart beat loudly as he observed Aadi. The symbolism of the scene wasn't lost on him. During the initial stages of a Theyyam performance, the artist gazes at a mirror after his physical transformation. This act of reflection, 'Mukha Darshanam', helps the performer invoke the deity and become one with God.

Saravanan remembered an old lesson he had learnt from Chindachchan about the art of Mukhamezhuthu, the intricate ritual of painting the artists' faces in dance forms like Theyyam. The white stripes, he said, cleared the mind and made it receptive to fear. Looking at Aadi, Saravanan felt he was living that lesson.

The roll of dice first landed on Nandanar, a worker at the local movie theatre. Nandanar had cleaned up the cinema hall after the late-night show and was returning home. To get home quickly, he crossed the bridge and was walking by the fields near the saline wetlands. It was a route he took regularly, so the pitch-black night, the rustling of leaves and the endless lonely stretch didn't bother him at all. He was walking jauntily, thinking about the injustices inflicted on him by his boss at the theatre and cursing him.

The paddy fields stretched out before him were made up of marshy land, water, dense thickets. There was not a sliver of fear in Nandanar's mind. As he traced his steps along a gravelly path among the slippery slush, he felt as comfortable as he would in his own home.

But at the end of the Sixth Corner, Saravanan waited on the jagged branches of a jackfruit tree.

Saravanan saw a dark shadow in the distance. He didn't recognise Nandanar, but he could make out the contours of a man. He hooted twice as a signal to Aadi. Aadi emerged from his hiding place behind a portia tree and began to walk on the same path as Nandanar.

Even from a distance, Nandanar could see that someone was walking towards him. He felt a surge of enthusiasm. Perhaps it was one of his acquaintances setting out on a fishing trip. He began to walk faster. As he got closer, he saw a man swaddled in a blanket. Something was off about his gait. He flashed a torchlight on the figure and glanced at the man's face. Then, he stood stunned, like the time he was stumped when a stone he had aimed at a mango tree hit a wasp's nest. He took about ten steps back. Screaming at the top of his lungs, he turned on his heels and fled with Aadi in hot pursuit, the edges of his blanket flying loose behind him.

As they faded out of sight, Saravanan slid down the tree with the agility of a bear. If their plan failed, Aadi would be in grave danger. The thought of the disgrace that could follow lacerated him. Panic made him move faster. He felt like he was flying; his legs seemed to have a life of their own.

Only after running for a long while did Nandanar have the courage to turn around. The sight he saw before him was bloodcurdling. That terrifying form was just an arm's length behind him. Nandanar gathered all his strength and began to sprint again.

But he couldn't sustain his dead run. He lost his balance and crashed his head against the low branch of a bola tree. Nandanar felt himself spinning as he hit the ground. He fell off the gravelled path but the soft marsh held him up like a bed, protecting him from serious injury.

The fall stopped Aadi in his tracks. As he got closer, Aadi realised that Nandanar was not in grave danger. He plucked a tender leaf from the bola tree and placed it on Nandanar's lips so that he would stay unconscious for a long time.

Saravanan was running towards them. He jumped off the path and landed on the marsh, splashing mud in all directions. Struggling to catch his breath, he looked down at Nandanar.

'What happened to him?' he gasped. Aadi could feel the shiver in his voice.

'Crashed against a tree … not injured or anything … Help me lift him. There's one more thing to do.'

Aadi pulled off his blanket and wrapped it around Nandanar.

Saravanan was behind Aadi as they held Nandanar by the arms and dragged him through the marsh. A few doubts crept up within Saravanan. But he reminded himself that he needed to have faith in Aadi. He brushed those thoughts away and turned his attention to the body they were hauling across the marsh.

'He's so bloody heavy … does he eat up all the money he makes?' Saravanan was struggling to stay upright on the slippery path. He could feel his knees giving way.

'Don't curse, my friend … Normal people eat. Not everyone lives on broken dreams like we do …' Aadi, too, was panting as he spoke. Saravanan went silent. As they walked through the inundated paddy fields, their footsteps sounded like fish wiggling about in water. Aadi was deep in thought. He hadn't taken up this job for the petty cash the brewers had offered him. He had a strategy. But how much of that did he want to reveal to Saravanan? Did he want to tell him the plan in one go? Or take him through it, step by step, as events unfolded? Even if Saravanan knew nothing, he would stand by Aadi. Eventually, a confused Aadi decided to confess when the time was right.

Like tiny ants struggling to transport a large prey, the two men traversed the marshland and the flood plains until they reached Peelimudi. They dropped Nandanar in the thickets before the dense forests began. They then sat on the branch of a nearby tree, their country revolvers in position. Aadi was adamant that no wild animal should attack Nandanar before he came to his senses.

Saravanan noticed Aadi on high alert, his eyes trained to spot any movement towards the body he was guarding. Man or beast, no hunter wanted his prey stolen, thought Saravanan.

It was a long wait. Nandanar came to after four hours. He felt disoriented, as if someone had whacked him on the head. When he tried to recollect what had happened, his mind dried up. As if a snake had wrapped itself around his leg. He could have dismissed what he had seen that night as a bad dream.

But he could not for the life of him figure out one thing. He remembered falling by the marshy fields. How did he reach so close to the Peelimudi forests? His thoughts and imagination went haywire. He used to be a man who wasn't afraid of anything but himself. Now, a slight breeze at Peelimudi, the movement of leaves, everything scared him. For four days, he was a shivering, feverish mess.

Nandanar was not just a worker at Shanthi Theatre. He was also the Kudakkaran of the local temple, the one chosen by heredity to hold up the umbrella for the deity. But it took four long days for the temple trustees and officials to visit him.

They walked in a single file as they entered Nandanar's small room. The last in the line was Kaatti, the *Andhithiriyan*, the priest who lit the oil lamp at the shrine. He was feeling guilty that they hadn't visited earlier.

It was a small room with a low door and a bed. Nandanar watched the visitors bending low to enter through the door, each a flower snapping away from its stalk. Despite his sorrows, he smiled.

The visitors were curious. 'Nanda … is it true, what they're saying?' Kudakkaran Raghavan already knew the gory details, but nothing beat the pleasure of hearing it all first-hand. He sat closer to Nandanar. Nandanar just smiled in reply.

Nandanar waited for Kaatti to come closer. He ensured that everyone was within hearing distance before he began his movie-style narration of events. He left out the parts where he had been frozen by terror. He exaggerated his bravery and courage. As he finished, he started to believe in his version of events and felt proud of himself.

Kaatti was contrite because he hadn't visited his friend earlier and he was in the mood for some flattery. 'In Chelari, a creature they were calling Blackman was on the prowl. But who could be brave enough to play such tricks in Ettunaad? That too with our arm-wrestling champion Nandanar?'

'What's the point if your forearms are the strongest? The mind should also be strong,' Raghavan tried to provoke Nandanar, hoping to hear more of the story, but Nandanar didn't bite. He gazed out of the window at a tree, its bark and branches showing early signs of scale insect infestation.

Even though the men were shirtless, the heat in the cramped room became oppressive within five minutes. They signalled to Kaatti that it was time to leave. There was no one to serve a cup of tea because Nandanar lived alone. Kaatti, too, felt there was no point in hanging around. Raghavan clung on like a leech for a little while, hoping to extract some more information, but finally lost his patience when Nandanar refused to budge. They left the room in the same order as they had come in. Raghavan threw in a taunt or two on his way out. Nandanar's heart felt heavy, as if a stone had been placed on his chest.

People quickly forgot about the incident. The village concluded that Nandanar was a coward and moved on to new stories.

Aadi was undeterred. 'That's okay … this is just the first blow. Keep up the strikes and even a grinding stone will give way,' he said to Saravanan. He had been cooking up new schemes to spread fear.

The next two days, relentless rain brought life in Ekarmala to a halt. People were afraid to step out. Rain lashed down like a rogue beast on Ettunaad, the hills, the forest and the fields. The older generation feared the return of another flood.

On the third day, the rain still came down in fits and starts. There was a slight drizzle when Gireeshan decided to go toddy tapping. He cautiously felt the bark of the coconut tree to check if it was slippery. He gingerly began to climb up the tree. He was first amused when he came across a few talismans and red threads tied around the trunk. He stopped to closely examine the threads. Were they signs of sorcery? He smiled at the foolishness of those who still believed in black magic in the twenty-first century. But his smile froze when he overturned the bamboo pot used to extract toddy. The pot was filled with blood. Gireeshan felt his body tighten, and a strange sense of panic spread from head to toe. He lost his grip and let out a scream that was drowned out by the sound of the rain as he fell down the tree like a coconut. He should have crashed down, like a shattered coconut inflorescence, but fate came to the rescue in the form of three bales of hay meant for the cows. He landed on the hay and fractured his thigh and arm.

Gireeshan's accident caused panic in the town. Even though he lived in the tiny hamlet of Velarkod, Gireeshan was popular across the valley of Ekarmala. The fact that both Gireeshan and Nandanar were from Velarkod led to some speculation.

The talk of the town was that there was a murky entity—an individual or a group—that was trying to spread fear in the relatively less populated areas of the region.

The idea of a neighbourhood watch gained ground. People from all eight villages started a night patrol in the region. Armed with flaming torches, stout sticks and jack knives, they ploughed through every bylane, alert for the slightest sign of mischief. Their searchlights, emergency lamps and torches ate up the darkness. They stood guard over Velarkod with their weapons through the night.

For sustenance, and to keep their spirits up, they made, makeshift woodfires by placing pairs of stones together.

Spicy chicken curry and rice bubbled over in pots when Raghavan began to talk about the old days. 'You know, Rahul, in our time, we never ate broiler chicken. All we got was spent hens.'

He was mixing the curry into the mashed rice as he tried to bond with his nephew.

'Would you make a curry out of it?' Rahul had his back to his uncle.

'We didn't have enough money to strut around like you did. No one had enough money. As soon as a hen stopped laying eggs, it was considered spent. We would grab the hen, kill it, and make a curry. It tasted funny if we cooked it at home. It was most delicious when we cooked it over an open fire pit like this.'

Raghavan felt the flavours of the past water his mouth. The phrase 'strut around' had offended Rahul, so he stayed focused on his food and was in no mood for chatter. By then, the sixth group had returned from their search. Nothing unnatural had been spotted. 'They would have disappeared knowing we were on the lookout. Whoever they are, surely they value their lives a little bit, right?' Saally quickly poured curry onto the mountain of rice on his plate. Even though Velarkod was noisy with all those people up and about, the night was calm.

Nothing happened as was expected. Nothing happened as was feared.

Death-o-Metre

The serpent of fear continued its slither through Velarkod. But Aadi made a dramatic decision to change the scene of action.

The brewers were happy with the commotion around Ekarmala. They were confident that they could manipulate Aadi to move in the direction of their choosing. Their leader, Satyajit, was curious to understand Aadi's modus operandi.

Aadi wanted to raise the bar. They had got this far without getting caught. The time was right. Young and able-bodied men turned up in full strength to join the search parties, combing the fringes of Velarkod. The fear of darkness was at its peak. By dusk, the rest of the villagers would hut themselves indoors.

The next roll of dice fell on Giripuram.

After her evening shower, Saranya, a young woman, double-checked if she had bolted the front door. She heard an unusual sound from the barn where the cows were tethered, something like the clip-clop of a horse's hooves. She wanted to find out where the sound was coming from and began to walk towards the barn. She was a few feet away when someone threw a noose around her neck.

The noose tightened. Saranya felt the breath seeping out of her body and her limbs thrashed about. Her attacker had no intention of killing her. He loosened the noose before she collapsed. The intruder made sure that she wasn't dead and disappeared into the darkness. She fell flat on the floor, foaming at the mouth.

Satyajit and the brewers were even more appreciative of Aadi as the news spread. But the incident was a lethal blow to the residents of Ettunaad. So far, the watch parties were almost festive what with the plates of chicken and rice. Now it was a question of life and death. They armed themselves with sticks and weapons, the desire for vengeance burning bright inside them.

Aadi and Saravanan led the group, stoking fear and anger. Aadi felt that they had to go the extra mile to appear innocent. Things would get out of hand if anyone in the crowd had even a sliver of suspicion about them.

As Saravanan had guessed, Aadi's ghostly disguise was not meant to help the brewers. Rajan's arrival had lit a fire under Aadi. For the first time, he saw the possibility of executing the grand plot he had nurtured for years. As events unfolded, Aadi decided it was time to move things his way. As he walked the long path through Ekarmala towards Velarkod, Aadi thought of his next steps.

The next day, Aadi ratted on the hooch distillers. He accused them of theft. Gold ornaments that had recently gone missing from the villages mysteriously turned up at the brewers' godown. Aadi joined the villagers and middlemen in beating up Satyajit and his men. Aadi's strongest blows landed on Rajan. By the time the police arrived from Thuravoor, the mob had walloped the brewers. Sticks, bricks, cattle ropes, and any weapon they could get their hands on had made a mark on the brewers' bodies.

Only a lathi-charge managed to disperse the crowd. The SI, who had recently taken charge, had heard that Ettunaad was a place that was considered a no-go area for cops. He looked around and perceived that Aadi was the leader of the group. He praised Aadi effusively and shared his phone number, with an invite to contact him in case of trouble.

Saravanan hoped things would end there. But Aadi now behaved like a feudal lord drunk on an unexpected boost of power.

One evening, he strutted around the saline fields and tumbled down his favourite mounds like an elephant gone rogue.

'We are moving to Ekarmala,' he proclaimed when he calmed down.

Saravanan remained poker-faced, but he was amused. He looked up at the Ekarmala hills. You talk as if we have a place to stay and the choice of moving homes! Stray dogs might choose to sleep outside a shop front one night and on the quay the next. Like the dogs, Aadi and Saravanan had no fixed address.

That night, Saravanan was full of doubts as he walked behind Aadi, all their belongings packed into two bags. He imagined that the cold water splashing against their heels as they walked through the swamp would slowly cool his fears.

The doctor said Saranya had had a narrow escape. The loose knot on the thick rope was what saved her. If the rope were any thinner, she would have collapsed, even if the knot hadn't killed her. Saranya didn't get better even after two days and two nights in the ICU. But the doctor continued to reassure the family that she would make it.

Saranya's father, Kangaani, hung around the hospital only during the day. As soon as it was dusk, he would go home and work according to a plan. He used a machine to hack away at the iron rods that held up an asbestos shed in his yard. '*Kreeeee* ...' The blades made a loud sound as they sliced into the hollow iron rods. He climbed up a ladder to reach the top of the rods and brought them down with a vengeance. Soon, there was a rain of pipes. Kangaani spared two pillars so the shed would still stand. He gathered the rest of them in a heap, the way logs of wood are gathered to make the Meleri, the fire pit for the Theyyam.

He lit a gas cutter with a lighter. He burned each pipe, shaping the edges like the mouths of the conical paper cups that peanut sellers use, and began filling the pipes to the brim with crushed stones. Then he welded the mouth of the pipes to close the cone. In the end, he had twenty heavy weapons. He carried each pipe as if it were a baby and loaded them all into his auto rickshaw.

Raghavan was impressed when he picked up the rods. 'This is good stuff ... Tough to carry, yes. But one strike, and you can split a man's head to pieces,' he said, wide-eyed.

The invigorated villagers let themselves loose on the Ekarmala hills that night. Groups of young men ventured into the edges of the Peelimudi forest. The treasures they brought back after their relentless search were meagre. Three boars, a piglet, a python trapped in a sack. Their prey came too easy that night. They grabbed what they found on their way. Eating game without the thrill of a hunt is no fun. The meat from the boars and the piglet was barely enough for a good pickle. Luckily, the snake was large enough, and it went into a simmering pot the next day.

In a corner of the hospital canteen, Ravi was cold as he nursed a frothy glass of pineapple juice. He was carrying a bag with two lakh rupees that Giridharan had sent him. He touched the bag gently, as if it were a pet bird, and then placed his hands on the smooth marble table. He felt the cold of the marble spread to his hands.

As he sipped on the juice, he imagined he was being transformed into a giant pineapple. His thorny exterior was sliced off and his core was being served on a plate, all sour and sweet. It was that lovely a day.

The bills for medicines and tests kept flowing in from the hospital. Saranya's family could not afford even a syringe. Her father, Kangaani, had spent a lifetime serving Achchan Namboodiri before they fell out. Now he made some money by helping the welder next door. He had a place to call home, a house built for him by Achchan Namboodiri, but he had no savings to his name. After Saranya's injury, the family was stressed about finding the means to get her proper treatment. That was when Giridharan made a call from Qatar to enquire about her. He offered to pay her hospital bills even before the family could put in a request.

In a blink, two lakh rupees were transferred to Ravi's account. Ravi could not make sense of it: Why would someone offer money to help a woman he hardly knew? That too, lakhs of rupees. Ravi absently moved his straw inside the empty glass. All he could think of was Giri.

'Your enemy Giri is now everyone's hero. Hasn't everything we did come to naught?' Saravanan tried to provoke Aadi as he cleaned a storage room for coconut husks at the cemetery around the bend in Ekarmala.

Aadi was busy clearing the cobwebs in the attic. 'That isn't a big deal,' he said.

Saravanan didn't give up. 'Now, he's going to be the hero.'

Aadi's voice resonated with self-confidence. 'Giri is like that short spot of sunshine that lights up a dark, rainy day. He will quickly fade into oblivion again.'

'Can't we go back to our old home? The house is disintegrating, with no one to care for it. Why do we have to live in a place like this?' Saravanan repeated a question he had asked Aadi many times over the years.

'It's not been abandoned. Aren't Kaanaadi and Kelachchan there? It isn't yet time for us to go back there,' Aadi, too, repeated his standard answer.

Ravi handed over thirty thousand rupees to Gireeshan, who was still bedridden after falling off the coconut tree. He was careful to remind the family about who their benefactor was. 'This is Giri's money. See me as the mere messenger who's delivering this to you. If not for me, then someone else would have delivered this to you. Consider this the largeness of a man's heart … what else can I say?'

Gireeshan held Ravi's hands, his fingers closing in tight. Ravi loosened his grip and walked away.

Gireeshan, the toddy tapper, was at peace. A long time ago, he had attacked Giridhar. At night, Giridhar had been found at the home of an Anganwadi teacher who was single. Gireeshan and his band of self-appointed moral guardians had tied Giridhar to a tamarind tree and beaten him senseless. When Giridhar unexpectedly came into a lot of money, Gireeshan had thought he would come for him. But he turned out to be the most helpful at a time of need.

Gireeshan clutched the bundle of cash and lay spread-eagled. Like a happy lottery seller laying out his wares on a blazing hot day.

Raghavan praised Giri to the skies as he dipped a piece of bread into the previous night's roasted snake curry. His nephew, Rahul, was next to him, fiddling with his glass of tea.

'Giri is now a Theyyam, a Thira, and all thanks to you. That's only because he entrusted you with the job of looking after his Udayapuram house. Everyone here knows what he's up to,' Rahul remarked.

Raghavan didn't say anything. He pushed a plate of banana chips and another plate of roasted snake towards Rahul, then gathered his umbrella and torch and bolted out of the house.

Balan, the tea-shop owner, spotted Raghavan through the dust-coated window of his kitchen and started to make Raghavan's favourite tea. Straining the tea through a sieve stiff with a week's worth of tea dust, Balan prepared Raghavan's black tea that stood out among the milk teas like a burnt-out ember. He gathered the glasses on a large tray and made his way to his customers.

The discussion was centred around Giri. Kuttan was narrating the story of Giri's ascent. 'He had a deal with the Arab woman here. He got lucky when her husband died in a lorry accident. The money and the lady landed on his lap. How else was he able to send across two lakh rupees for a minor case of hanging? All thanks to the Arab's wife, Arab's money! He doesn't have to think much before spending.'

Raghavan wasn't pleased with this version of the story. 'A lorry accident? Was her husband a truck driver that he would die in a lorry? If you don't know the truth, just shush … Let *me* tell the story. One time, when the Arab was reversing his car, his little boy—he was only as old as our Vasanthi's son then—almost got crushed under the wheels. Giri pledged his life to save the boy. The car went over Giri's foot, and a bone splintered into four.' Raghavan sipped a bit of tea, then added, 'Moreover, Giri considers the Arab's wife as his own mother.'

'Mother?! Don't stretch it that far, Ettan Mooppare … Mooshaari says that she is only twenty years old. Mother, he says!' Kuttan tore off a large piece of double omelette and shoved it into his mouth.

Raghavan dropped his glass on the table and turned menacingly towards Kuttan. 'You think the Arab is going to display his wife's age and colour before Mooshaari when he passes by? Don't overdo this.'

Kuttan raised his voice: 'It's not like you've seen her.'

The people around were gleeful, waiting for a fistfight. Balan, who was stacking up the previous day's banana fritters, turned around to see what would happen next.

At that moment, Kaatti, the lighter of lamps at the temple, walked into the shop. No one was expecting him. Everyone froze for a second, and then the scene got calmer. Raghavan and Kuttan retreated. It was as if a Theyyam had walked into the arena—everyone went back to their allotted seats.

At the cemetery, Saravanan lay on a blanket spread on a casket. He was restless. He could not figure out why Aadi had tried to kill Saranya with the rope. Aadi avoided the question whenever he asked. Neither could he understand why Aadi had snitched on the brewers when they were paying him and Aadi a good sum of money. Even after the brewers had been driven away, Aadi continued his schemes to frighten people. Saravanan knew he had been plotting away. Aadi neither told Saravanan his plans nor did he ask Saravanan for an opinion. Aadi, Saravanan thought, sought vengeance on everyone. Sometimes, he behaved like a possessed man.

Saravanan used to think that life was passing him by. If you cannot live life fully in your youth, he thought, when will you ever savour life? There had been times earlier, too, when Aadi had schemed and executed various plans without confiding in Saravanan. But all those plots ended well for them, and only later did Saravanan get the full picture. Those were relatively small moves. Now, Aadi was playing with fire. A small misstep and the entire mob would turn against them. Worrying thoughts continued to buzz around Saravanan's head through the night.

Kaatti left Balan's tea-shop, lit lamps surrounding the temple, and was on his way back home. Dusk was giving way to night but there was still a glimmer of light left in the sky. He climbed down the steep path after the Chekkyampara bend and strolled down the road. He raised his head to the left when he sensed some movement in a thicket of ixora flowers.

He saw a pair of hands swiftly picking flowers. Kaatti guessed it was a local Theyyam performer, and he moved off the road to check. He called out when he was unable to make out who was there. The man raised his head to look at Kaatti and then bent down. He lowered his painted face among the flame-red flowers. Kaatti caught a glimpse of the face. Fear slinked through him. A scream got stuck in his throat. He felt his head go numb and everything went dark before his eyes. He held on to his thighs for support but fell into the slush with all the grace of a banana tree felled by a strong wind.

The Roar of Chindan

Kaatti lay unconscious in the slush until Mooshaari and Kuttan spotted him. They shook him awake. Kaatti dragged himself home but he couldn't sleep that night.

At the break of dawn, Kaatti returned to Chekkyampara to inspect the spot where he had fallen. The ixora flowers had been plucked delicately. The stems had suffered no damage. The buds and tender flowers had been spared. He inspected four flower beds, and he instinctively knew that it was Chindachchan whom he had seen the previous night.

Chindan, the lion! Kaatti felt the needle prick of fear running along his body.

The news spread like wildfire. Curious onlookers squeezed into the tiny courtyard of the temple. But that evening, Kaatti wasn't on duty as the temple Andhithiriyan, the one whose job was to light lamps around the temple.

He was laid up in bed with a fever. Soon, the tide of people gushed into the yard of Kaatti's tiny house. The little house with decaying gable roof tiles had been built for him by the temple authorities. Kaatti, who was in no mood to meet anyone, had bolted his doors shut.

Some people in the crowd wanted to break in forcefully but then felt that it would be way out of line. They split into small groups, still circling the house in the hope of some news.

Arjun stood with his hand on his friend Rahul's shoulders. 'Too bad it's a temple official's house … Else, we could have broken the door down and asked him what happened.' Everyone had their own theory on what had transpired.

Kuttan and Mooshaari were severely disappointed that they weren't able to ferret out information as soon as Kaatti came to his senses. Kuttan thought Kaatti had fainted because he had skipped a meal. Kaatti, too, didn't volunteer any information. The next day, Mooshaari took Kuttan aside at the club and told him about the rumours floating around. Only then did Kuttan understand that there was a ghostly angle to the story.

At the tea-shop, Balan set down a glass of steaming tea in front of Kangaani. 'Kaatti just escaped by a rat's whisker. He was lucky that Chindachchan didn't take revenge on him for what happened in the past,' he said.

Kangaani, who had been staring at the peeling walls around him, was taken aback. He pushed aside the glass and stared intently at Balan.

'Balaa … this is 2020. And you're taking comfort in the fact that a ghost did not harm anyone? Are you crazy?' His words were laced with contempt.

Balan didn't budge. 'I think you yourself are very scared, Kangaani!'

Kangaani wasn't expecting that response. He had no answer, and to avoid talking, he took a long sip of hot tea. His tongue and throat burned. He spat out the boiling liquid back into the glass.

Kuttan had been reading the paper and listening in from a corner. 'A mere mention of that name, and you're flabbergasted! Who knows what else is going to come next? Forget what was done to the man before his death. That's a nasty deed unworthy of gossip even at a casual gathering. And did you all leave him alone even after the man was dead and gone? The Kodiyila that should rightfully go to Chindachchan's heir … isn't that what you are giving to that newly rich fellow, Giri? Even though Aadi knows he will not get what should be his, he comes prepared, bathed and fresh, every year after the third Kaliyaattam. My heart breaks when Giri's wife, Praseetha, receives the Kodiyila and smugly walks away … You have snuffed out a family's light. No matter how many lamps you burn now, no matter how many times you walk clockwise around a temple, you can't escape what you did. Go back and check your accounts. You will receive a fair share of trouble for everything you did.' Kuttan folded his newspaper into two, placed it on another table, and walked away.

Balan had always considered Kuttan a bit asinine but, this time, he thought Kuttan had a point. Balan sat on an old, broken chair at his shop and thought of the old days. Saravanan was an excellent student. He went to school along with his son, Dhanal, and would visit them often. Aadi and Saravanan were both good boys back then. It was only after the death of Chindachchan that they went astray.

Kangaani sat still at his table, but his mind was a mess. He didn't believe the gossip. Even if Chindachchan were to hunt him down, there were many others who had done the dead man more harm: Raghavan, Giri, Achchan Namboodiri. Kangaani thought he was the last in a long queue anyway. There was no point in fuming at the bow when the archer was standing right in front of you, was there?

Mooshaari was upset at not getting Kaatti's version of the event, even though he had him at arm's length. Kaatti had locked himself out of the world. Mooshaari could have become a hero if only he had probed a bit further. Even if he had got just a few words out of Kaatti, he could have used his vivid imagination and spun wild tales that would have lasted at least two weeks. He did ask Kaatti why he had fainted. But Kaatti hadn't been very forthcoming. Mooshaari didn't want to trouble the Andhithiriyan any further, so he stopped bothering him. What a big blunder! He could feel his head swell. He didn't join the search party that night. Instead, he spent all his time thinking about what he could do next, and he finally came up with a solution.

The next morning, he found a strategic spot at the tea-shop. He let out that Kaatti wasn't the only one who had seen Chindachchan. He had also got a glimpse. No one bought his story.

'Fools like you will never get the chance to see Chindachchan,' Balan said as he gathered the used plates.

Mooshaari didn't receive the reactions he had expected, but he didn't falter. He dipped into his imagination and pulled out strands of stories, hoping something would stick. Balan kept mocking his attempts. You say something in all seriousness, and everyone around considers it a joke. A lesser man would have given in. But Mooshaari was undeterred. The taunts slid off him. Balan felt he was drumming a chenda, the percussion instrument used in a Theyyam performance. He beat the sticks hard but there was no sound because the drumhead was worn and loose from repeated usage.

'I don't care if no one believes me. I was the first one to see Kaatti after he fell. Before I could reach him, a man with a large cloth bag passed by on my left. I can't tell you for sure that it was Chindachchan. To tell you the truth, I didn't even notice his face. But I am sure of one thing. Many parts of his body were burnt.' Mooshaari took care to show no visible signs that he was lying and stopped at that critical point in the story.

A man with a burnt body. Everyone in the room felt the heat as if they were standing before the giant fire pit during a Theyyam. The glass in Balan's hand felt as light as a raindrop. Before he knew it, it had slipped through his fingers, shattering to pieces. The others felt like they had been handed down a boiling hot vessel they couldn't hold on to. By noon, the news had circulated all over Ettunaad, and once more, there was an outbreak of fear. But the day wasn't over yet. Saranya passed away, not willing to wait until the wounds on her neck healed. A sad day made way for dusk.

Saranya's death. Kaatti's fall. Mooshaari's mendacious tale. Even the search parties were afraid to venture out after the flood of bad news. The children of Ettunaad were anxious: What new terror the darkness would bring? Maybe their fear was a portent of the darkness ahead.

Two nights later, the embers of mistrust and fear threatened to turn into a conflagration.

Kangaani was consumed with the goal of seeking revenge against those who had killed his daughter. Normally, bereaved family members stay away from community activities for sixteen days until funeral rituals are over. However, Kangaani turned up the very next day after his daughter's cremation to lead the nightly neighbourhood watch. The search party split into small groups. Most of the young men rallied behind Kangaani, eager to show their support. They climbed down Ekarmala and headed towards Udayapuram. Kangaani walked along a pathway washed by rainwater on the edge of the hill, taking care not to slip. Suddenly, he saw a strange sight by the swamps at the foot of the hill. He stopped right in his tracks. Aadi had hatched a new plan for this night a few days ago. High on hooch, he was lying down on a bed of coconut husks when he shared the idea with Saravanan. They set the plan in motion.

They braided together dried coconut leaves to make a flaming torch and got two pots that were normally used to extract toddy into.

Now, Saravanan waited by the foot of Ekarmala, where the marshland ended. Aadi began his run towards Ekarmala, holding the flaming torch high up. Periodically, he dipped the torch into one of the pots. After a few steps, he held up the torch again, fanning it against the wind to light up the coconut leaves. He waved the torch and then put it back in the pot. When he reached the middle of the swampy fields, he stopped and doused the torches with water. Then it was Saravanan's turn. He began running up Ekarmala with the torch flying high.

Kangaani, leading from the front, was the first in the search party to spot what looked like a flame that kept appearing on and off at will. Suddenly, he felt like an unfortunate voyager facing sky-high waves, unsure of what to do. The people behind him held their breath. From where they stood, it seemed like a giant ball of fire was rushing towards them. The crowd huddled together when the flame disappeared for a while. In a blink, the fire was back, seeming to rise higher and higher on the hill.

Kangaani was the first to scream. The crowd scattered like a herd of stray dogs startled by a stone. In just a minute, the search party that had been marching in a neat file became a disjointed mess.

Apart from the vagaries of age, Kangaani was a healthy man. But he was afraid to run through the rubber plantations. Long ago, Shashi Ettan had been found hanging near a well in the middle of the plantation. Just like today, Kangaani had led a search party in Ekarmala to find the body. He was present when Mooshaari had lowered the body. Since that day, he had been afraid to walk anywhere close to the rubber trees.

So he crossed the pump house and ran towards the cremation ground. He increased his pace and then slowed down. The sound of the wind and his memories seemed to be his only companions. Suddenly, he had a hunch that he was being followed. He climbed down the stone bund and ran through a path overgrown with wild creepers. He saw a glowing spark of fire coming towards him as if someone had blown the fire his way. Then, the spark faded away in the dark. Kangaani lost his balance and fell. He managed to heave himself up. Turning around, he began to run again, his legs flying over the fresh slush.

He hit an overgrown rubber branch and crashed, head-first, into the stone bund. Struggling to his feet, he walked a few steps ahead but kept falling repeatedly due to exhaustion. Now near the smokehouse where heaps of rubber sheets were stacked and hung out to dry, he tried to keep moving.

It wasn't the fall that killed him. Someone pushed him into a dead, unused well behind the smokehouse. He fell to the bottom of the well. In the dark, his blood mingled with the shallow water in the well. Jeetu, who was behind Kangaani, heard the thud of a fall and the scream that followed.

A Forest in Bloom on the Riverbank

Kalesh sat on the marshy riverbank, watching his father bobbing around in circles in the water. His father, Narayanan, resembled a freshwater mullet captured in a bottle.

Narayanan came up for air and spat out the river from his mouth. 'Are you sure you saw Saravanan empty the cage?' he asked, referring to the bamboo basket they used to trap fish from the river.

Kalesh dug a clenched fist into the damp soil. 'How many times do I have to tell you? Yes! I saw him empty the bamboo cage and take out all the fish. For a month, we haven't been getting any fish, not even baby fish, no matter where we set up the bamboo trap. I had been suspecting foul play for a week. So, I hid high up on a coconut tree. That was the only way I could have caught him. What a surprise! And what's more—I kept shifting the location of the cage underwater because we weren't getting any fish. Each time, he knew where the cage was and stole the fish. For the life of me, I couldn't figure out how he knew where exactly I had set the trap. He's as thin as a rail, but he has enough poison inside him to fill two big drums!'

'Don't underestimate him because of his size,' his father warned as he waded to the shore. 'True, he's only an earthworm. But if you set the bait, the one who bites will be Aadidev. Now that one, Aadi, he's a cobra! To hell with the two of them! Stealing our fish, moving our cage … that is child's play to him. His father was Chindan Shingam, the Lion. He could climb tall trees and snare a bird in flight. Aadi has been planting the seeds of vengeance within Saravanan. In any case, the apple doesn't fall far from the tree.'

Narayanan stepped on a fallen coconut trunk and washed his feet. The silt he had carried from the river flowed back into the water. The river shimmered with an otherworldly beauty. It was quiet, and except for a stationary boat in the distance, there was no one around. Narayanan glanced at the boat and made his way towards Kalesh.

'Acha, I don't know why you are so scared of them. Are you saying that we should bow down to some Tamil woman's son, and simply watch while he steals from us?'

Narayanan didn't answer. He shook his towel to dry it, picked up his bamboo cage, and walked away. An infuriated Kalesh stomped his foot in the slush.

Late that night, Aadi and Saravanan were hacking away at a tree with saws. Saravanan let go of the saw, cracked his knuckles, and climbed onto a higher branch.

'I'll be honest. I don't understand what we are doing. Why did Kangaani have to die? Why are we killing people? Who benefits from what we do? Are we going to settle scores with blood for every past crime? Where do you think we'll end up with that approach? Have you ever thought about it?' Saravanan asked.

Aadi loosened his grip on the saw and edged towards the branch's end for a better view of Saravanan.

'We want the Kodiyila back. I will do anything for that. And you call this bloody? This is merely the bugle call to war. I am only just beginning,' Aadi replied.

That Kodiyila again! Receiving the Kodiyila was one of the most important prefatory rites before a Theyyam. On the day of the performance, a temple priest would hand over the Kodiyila—lighted wick-lamps on a banana leaf—to the Theyyam. The belief was that the Pujari invoked the spirit of the deity and infused it into the flames. After the performance, the artiste would return the Kodiyila to the priest. The act signified that the spirit of God was now back in the temple.

Saravanan ran his fingers along the bark of the tree. 'How exactly would Kangaani's falling into a well bring the Kodiyila back to us? What is the connection between his death and the Kodiyila?'

'This is a long game. Right now, it may be hard to see obvious connections between minor events. But you don't have to feel guilty about what we are doing. You and I are just the oxen that pull the cart. Chindachchan is the one who is travelling in the cart. Chindan Shingam!'

Aadi looked up to check Saravanan's reaction. In the darkness, he couldn't see Saravanan's expression. He could only see the outline of his twig-like figure. Aadi thought about Saravanan's emaciated frame. After the murder of Chindachchan, starvation had become their constant companion. Saravanan's waist was very narrow, as if someone had tightened a rope around him and shrunk him. The young man didn't even eat the little food that they got. Joy had disappeared from his life along with Chindachchan. After the murder, nothing enthused or interested him. A lean body with bones sticking out. Added to that was his servile body language: he bent before people as if waiting for orders. If he had had facial hair, he would have looked like a lunatic. Luckily, the only hair on his face was a thin moustache. A beard had never taken root on his face. Aadi needed to focus on Saravanan's health. But he would be able to get to it only after keeping the lit Kodiyila and a sword in front of Chindachchan's photograph. He needed to bequeath all rights to Chindachchan's old house and land to Saravanan alone. He wanted Saravanan to marry and raise children. But all that was for later. After the war was won and the weapons were gone, he would finally relax and think about the future. An armed man could not afford any distractions.

When he realised he was wasting time thinking these thoughts, Aadi abruptly straightened up. Saravanan followed his lead, and soon the sound of sawing filled the air. Sawing on wet wood in a certain rhythm can sound like the hissing of a barn owl. So, no one came to investigate. Aadi's technique was to chop down the tree slowly, taking enough time before it was cut off by the roots. Chop a tree off in one swoop, and everybody notices. The bark, branches and leaves were lowered into a nearby stream. The following night, they would travel through the river with the wood. If they started the transportation at 2 a.m., they could reach the old Velarkod factory by 3.30 a.m. They would store the wood there. When there was enough to fill a lorry, the wood would be taken to Payyannur.

The return journey from the Velarkod bank to the river's edge was always pleasant.

Like a broken wedding necklace, the Vannathi river gracefully encircled Velarkod and Udayapuram. It then twisted its way through dense banks, where bamboo baskets were often set deep in the waters to snare fish. Aadi and Saravanan liked to steal all the bigger, plump fish. At certain spots, Aadi knew he would find shiny, large fish nestled along the edges of the baskets. What a sight! It always made him feel as if he was gazing upon a lush forest blooming on the distant shores of a river.

After Saravanan submerged the wood in the brook, he was abuzz with excitement. His mind was already occupied with their upcoming expedition the following night. Meanwhile, Aadi held onto the wall as he navigated a slippery path. Suddenly, he turned around, his brows furrowed in deep thought.

'The Vannathi river,' he said, 'is nourished not only by its mighty tributaries and meandering streams but also by the gentle raindrops that trickle down the leaves and fall into its waters. The tragedy of our society lies in its failure to grasp this fundamental truth.'

Saravanan, who was walking behind him, couldn't fathom that statement. He wanted to change the subject.

'Aren't some sunrises particularly pretty?' Saravanan spread out his arms and felt the moss on the wet walls.

Aadi agreed. 'Yes, some days are good. For a hardworking man, daybreak is always pleasurable.'

On Aadi's shoulders was the heavy sack of tools that they had used to lower the wood into the brook. He knew that the cemetery might be crowded because of Kangaani's cremation later in the day, so he did not want to go there. When they came to the third brook, they took out ropes from the sack and tied them under the bridge above the brook. Then they hung the sack with axes, sickles and saws on the ropes.

Aadi kicked away the slimy mullet fish that were pecking at his ankles in the water, and they climbed their way up from the brook.

'We'll eat something at Balettan's shop. Let's not go home just yet. There will be a lot of people there,' he said, bending down to scratch his feet.

He moved, taking large strides forward, and Saravanan hurried to catch up with him but was beside himself with laughter. Had Aadi just referred to the cemetery as their 'home'?

At the tea-shop, Balakrishnan was holding forth on the town's hottest topic.

'Saravanan's mother, Kannagi, arrived here when they were rebuilding the temple gatehouse. She was part of the group of Tamil workers who came to construct the pillar sculptures. She was pregnant with Aadi when Chindachchan met her. Then, there was one more cursed offspring: Anand. He was Saravanan's own brother. God alone knows in which hell he is living now. Or else, like people have been saying ...'

Balan saw Aadi and Saravanan pass the temple wall to approach his shop, and stood up from his desk.

'They're headed this way. Lucky, I saw them! If that Aadi hears me speak anything about their family, he'll burn my shop down.'

'Didn't Kannagi have any family of her own, Baletta?' Shyamjeet asked while cooling down his tea.

'Yes, she had a younger brother, Kodumudi. He's an even bigger rascal than Aadi. I'll tell you later. If you talk too much now, you'll have to eat that parotta with your blood, not with that mackerel curry in front of you,' Balan said, using the white, handloom towel on his shoulder to wipe his desk, and rushed outside.

Aadi handed over a large basket of freshwater fish. 'Baletta, you look like you've been badmouthing us!'

'Who … me? Badmouthing Chindachchan's children? We were only discussing the situation here … Look at what's happening in our village. Isn't our town now a slaughterhouse!'

After Saravanan too stepped inside the shop, Balan raised the basket to check the freshness of the fish. He was satisfied.

Aadi sat on one of the benches, as wobbly as a child's wooden horse, and took measure of the room. He smiled weakly at Shyamjeet. He noticed a young stranger sitting alone in a corner. Around thirty years old. A sufficiently muscular body. He shoved the saltshaker off the table and bent down to pick it up. He noticed the man's shoes. When Aadi straightened up, he saw Kuttan sitting at another table. Their eyes met. Kuttan nodded, understanding Aadi's silent question.

Aadi had no appetite. The fish head lying in the deep waters of the mackerel curry reminded him of a broken raft. He didn't eat the fish but dipped the parotta in the curry and made a show of eating. After they had paid their bill, Balan came to clear the table. Aadi's glass of tea lay untouched, still steaming hot. About two minutes after they left, the stranger got up to leave. He glanced at the untouched glass of tea and said goodbye to Balan on his way out.

When Kuttan reached the cemetery, the rituals were over. The flames were starting to eat up Kangaani's body. He wriggled through the crowd and finally caught sight of Aadi. Aadi stayed put by the fire, kindling the flames when necessary. Kuttan hung around like a courtier forced to make his presence felt. Aadi noticed him only after a long time. He slipped out and stood next to Kuttan.

'I don't know in what disguise he is here. But one thing is certain: he is a cop. Look at his shoes and you will recognise he is a cop. That's why I asked you to investigate who he is.' Aadi talked in a low voice as they made their way out and walked towards the room where coconut husks were stored.

When they reached a quiet corner, Kuttan found a shady spot against the wall. Aadi's amiable face showed signs of stress.

'Do you know why he is here?' Aadi asked softly.

Kuttan folded one of his legs backward and leaned against the wall. 'No … To find out too much too soon would be foolishness. He'll get suspicious.'

'True that!' Aadi put his arm round Kuttan's shoulder. 'We must be very careful. If he were an intelligent officer, he would have booked us by now.'

Kuttan observed that Aadi's voice was laced with disappointment and irritation. He tried to comfort Aadi. 'Why are you overthinking this? Whatever has happened here so far cannot be directly linked to us.'

Aadi looked at the funeral pyre blazing at a distance. 'There is one link. Fire …'

Kuttan, too, turned to look at the flames. Since the top part of the pyre was covered, sparks escaped through various hollow spaces below.

'Do we need to do anything against him?'

Aadi twirled his moustache. 'There's no point doing anything now. We can't do anything to stop a man on a mission. We will do whatever a man is forced to do when faced with a strong adversary. But it's not yet time for that. When the time comes, we won't hesitate. Our soil has seen so much bloodshed. It can easily soak up one more stranger's blood.'

'Okay … let's see what time throws at us … For now, let Chindachchan be victorious.' Kuttan folded up his mundu and went downhill through the rubber plantation.

By the time Aadi returned, the flames had licked up the last of Kangaani's bones. He hung around with the family until the flames turned into ashes. After everyone left, he went to the coconut husk shed and lay down next to Saravanan.

Saravanan sat up. 'I've heard that Naranathu Bhranthan used to spend a lot of time in cemeteries.'

Naranathu Bhranthan. The madman of Naranath. The most famous eccentric in Kerala folklore, who is considered a seer and a prophet today. The story went that Naranathu Bhranthan would transport large boulders to the top of a hill. The rocks would be so big and the hill so steep that when he pushed a rock one foot up, it would roll down two feet. After a bloody, slow trek to the top, he would kick the boulder downhill and laugh aloud, clapping his hands. Unlike Homer's Sisyphus, Naranath wasn't a cursed man. There were many interpretations of why he did what he did. Some said it was a metaphor for the tendency of humans to work hard, hoping to enjoy the fruits of their labour in the future, unmindful of the possibility of death—a rock rolling down the hill. Others said he was trying to show how hard it was to rise in life and how easy it was to fall and perish.

Aadi wiped the sweat off his brow. 'When Naranathu Bhranthan rolled a rock down the hill, the people below were unharmed. If we were to do the same, a lot of flag bearers would get crushed into the soil. We are not Naranathu Bhranthan. We are the forces that live in graveyards. We are like Lord Shiva.'

After ninety minutes of practice, George Alex lay upturned like a fallen leaf on the water. It had been a long time since he had swum in a river, and he was enjoying the welcome change from a swimming pool. In a dreamy state of mind, he looked at the sky through the clear water. A sound interrupted him. A large raft whooshed past with all the speed of a race boat. The faces of those on the raft weren't clear. But in the moonlight, he had a clear vision of a certain weapon they carried in their torn sack. The sight made him alert. He was a tad disappointed that the clues he was seeking could surface without much effort on his part. He could hear Anand swimming towards him with clumsy, loud strokes.

Anand held onto a floating log, gasping for breath. 'Sir, some people are illegally transporting wood through the river.'

'Anand, did you notice anything unusual?'

'No, sir … their faces are covered.'

George ruminated on Anand's reply and floated downstream with the tide.

Kangaani's death was a rude shock. No one dared to venture out on the night of his funeral. The search party was off, but Rahul felt compelled to do something. He created a WhatsApp group for the young men in the locality: Puram Vendhrans. He sent an introductory message urging members to add friends and stay vigilant. In thirty minutes, the first text dropped. It was a photograph. A body with flesh clawed out. The face was intact. Rahul was so shocked that he put his phone away. The face seemed familiar to him. Curious, he summoned some courage and opened the image again. A chunk of flesh was missing from the left side of the body, with a red cloth stuffed into the gaping wound. Rahul's eye travelled above the neck. The phone slipped out of his hands. The man in the picture was Kalesh's father, Narayanan.

The Blazing Kodiyila

Purapuri Temple, 2017

Kaatti brushed the mud off his heels and furtively entered the temple gatehouse. He took off the thin cloth covering his upper body and dusted a spot where he wanted to sit. He hoped to escape the attention of temple authorities and elders.

The flame on a pillar lamp was unsteady. Korachchan put his palm over it, adjusted the wick till the flame was strong, and stepped back. He looked daggers at Kaatti.

'The official lighter of lamps is here … Can we begin now, Ravietta?' Achchan Namboodiri sought permission from the crowd with a symbolic gesture.

The air crackled with tension. The representatives of the Ettunaad Council had gathered to make a crucial decision. Should the Kodiyila, the grand symbol that signified the divine power handed to the Theyyam, go to a family that had performed at the temple for generations? Or should the invite go to an upstart who had agreed to pay a large sum of money for a much-needed temple renovation?

The officiator announced the names of the eight towns of Ettunaad: Velarkod, Giripuram, Udayapuram, Udayagiri, Ulinoor, Elavankottu, Perunthatta and Pormudi. The representatives of these towns then came forward: Vaduthala Kannan, Cheriya Veettil Koran, Verpuli Koran, Narayanan Mooppar, Palat Kannan, Raghavan, Pachchila Koranachchan and Ettillam Kannan Mooppar.

At the back row, Mooshaari whispered to Suran, 'I know we're not supposed to gossip about temple officials, but I can't resist it. Who does this Kaatti think he is? We have all been waiting for an hour. All he had to do was come up front and apologise for being late. Such a pompous fellow!'

Vaduthala Kannan, representing Velarkod, was the first to speak. 'We don't think we could raise ten lakhs for such a purpose. Our town has so few labourers and office workers. When someone agrees to give us this sum, we shouldn't turn our back on them. That's like jumping over the wall to enter a house when the gate is wide open. None of us have any objection to this. If the rules need to be adjusted, let's do that. Velarkod is ready to pull its weight. We will contribute our share of manual labour.'

The Giripuram representative chimed in, 'We are with Velarkod here.'

Cheriya Veettil Koran raised his hand and spoke with theatrical gestures. 'I don't understand why there should be a big discussion over this. Handing over the Kodiyila is NOT a traditional rite. I don't remember witnessing this ritual in our childhood. When Chindan croaked … sorry, when he died, the Kodiyila was given to his heirs as a sort of compensation. Giridharan is willing to give us ten lakhs to copperplate the temple chamber roof and construct sheds near the wall. All he asks in return is the Kodiyila. If it were someone else, wouldn't they have demanded ownership of the entire temple? I am not saying this because Giri is from our village. Of course, he is our pride. But more than that, we want to develop this temple. The Kodiyila should go to Giri.' Koran's body was shrivelled, but his voice was strong.

'Which compensation are you talking about? Four grains of rice, a few pieces of areca nut, and a burning wick placed on a banana leaf? That's not called compensation. Which world are we living in?' Mooshaari continued his whisper campaign, moving closer to Suran.

A brahminy kite glided high in the sky, looking down with curiosity. The group of people huddled in the courtyard looked like bundles of cut grass lying in the corner of a freshly mowed field. The kite flew lower and started circling the temple courtyard.

The crowd expected a fiery speech from Verpuli Koran. But he kept it muted and short: 'Everyone knows we are residents of the region that houses this grand temple. We have given our sweat and blood to this land. We stand with whatever the elders think is right. Any decision that is taken at this spot will only be for our own good.'

Narayanan Mooppar, who had been looking at the large kite, jumped in. 'Verpuli Koran's optimism seems to be backed by the heavens! Look at that holy kite circling over us. That's a sign. If we could give out two Kodiyilas there wouldn't be a problem at all. But astrological calculations warn against that. Astrologers have found signs that the sacred forces of this temple aren't too happy. If I may remind you all of what was revealed in the Swarna Prashnam, a lot of the seniors here would be miffed. The signs are indicating that the gods want women to do the heavy lifting here, not the muscular men. What a disgrace! In our modern age if our temple doesn't look good enough, it tells on the incapability of us, the men folk. Historically, we were a valiant people. Our ancestors stood where we are today, preparing to go to the forest and bring back a tiger. They were strong and courageous people. History is never written by those who bow and scrape. History travels through those whose chests are puffed out. We can regain some of our lost glory by refurbishing and cleaning up the temple. So many people are here, hoping to see a good fight. But even if ten thousand people gather, we cannot raise ten lakh rupees. Nobody is asking for a transfer of temple documents. Only for a piece of banana leaf. Are we saying we cannot provide a wick to keep on the leaf? Or that we don't have enough oil for the wick? Tell us what you lack, and we will bring it from Udayagiri. Chindan was a Theyyam performer because he was paid for it. He didn't do it for free. If you were to count the cost of the banana bunches Chindan's family has taken from the temple premises, it would be enough to copperplate ten temples. How will we get better? Some people here think that watering the vaar tree in the temple courtyard is development. Others boast that Giri is from their town. Is that something to boast about? We, the people of Ettunaad, are one unit. Otherwise, even we could boast that Giri's wife Praseetha is from our town. Why have an Ettunaad villages council otherwise? We suggest that Giri be informed of our assent. Let him bring in the tiles tomorrow to start the work.'

Narayanan Mooppar ended his speech only after someone tugged at his hand. He then dissolved into the crowd.

Next, it was Palat Kannan's turn. He adjusted the cloth on his upper body. 'Respectful greetings to the temple authorities and to the Ettunaad Council. If Narayanan had made these statements outside the temple premises, we would have chopped up his liver and wrapped it in a banana leaf. Only then would we have left for Ulinoor.' The people behind him yelled cries of encouragement.

'We haven't planted a mere coconut sapling in the temple courtyard. It is part of our lore that the vaar tree be planted here because it is a favourite of the Theyyam. These Udayagiri people … forget the current lot, take ten generations of their men. None will be able to get the seeds of this tree even if they scour the Peelimudi forests for a lifetime. They are only fit to boil spent hens in pots. Our brave kids went deep into the forest to get the right sapling. What's the need to be so dismissive of the tree!'

Avinash, the 'brave' soul who had got the sapling sat at the back with his chest puffed up. After all, no one would ever know the truth behind his expedition to the forest. He had gone to hide marijuana in the hollow of a tree when he saw the vaar tree. Mistaking it for a boli tree, he had brought the sapling home.

Kannan closed his speech: 'We would be proud if this temple got a facelift in our lifetime. If we get the money from Giri, and if we all pitched in four lakh rupees, we could use interlocking bricks across the building. Our temple would become a major attraction by the next Theyyam season.'

The next speaker, Raghavan, wrapped up his opinion within a few words: 'We think the Kodiyila should be given to Giri. It has an unseen benefit, too. If Giri gets the Kodiyila, he would be in constant touch with the temple's affairs. With enough financial backing, the worthy gentlemen in this group could take this temple to a whole new level. I don't think there is a need for any debate here.'

The Perunthatta representative interjected. 'People have waited for long and are fatigued. I don't want to make you wait longer. The Kodiyila ritual should take place as it always did. Shingam's heirs should get the Kodiyila. I don't need to go into the details of how Shingam died. Everyone assembled here knows the truth. I know many will disagree. But we are against giving the Kodiyila to a new family.' There was pin-drop silence when Pachchila Koran ended his speech.

'We agree with Palat Kannan. We can organise funds to refurbish the temple. We have brought one and a half lakh rupees from Pormudi.' At Kannan Mooppar's signal, two young men came forward with a bundle of cash wrapped in a dhoti.

Kuttan, who was part of the crowd, was frustrated by then. He folded his mundu and walked out in a huff. Outside in the sweltering heat, four people were waiting for him in the shade of a gooseberry tree: Saravanan, Kaanaadi, Aadi and Kelachchan.

'Kuttan, what happened?' Saravanan asked, with no trace of hope in his voice.

'Come. Let's go. If we wait any further, we will have to witness them giving away the sword and the throne, too, to Giri,'

The four men didn't probe further. They walked behind Kuttan in a single file. Raghavan, who was standing by the temple wall, saw Kaanaadi, hobbling on a stick, leading the pack. He burst out laughing. 'The five Pandavas! Everybody is here. Are you here to claim the kingdom for yourself?'

Inside, Achchan Namboodiri addressed the crowd after the representatives had had their say. 'In case anyone has a different opinion, please speak up now.'

Mooshaari, seated right at the back, summoned courage. 'We are talking about Gulf money … Do you think it is right to use the money of non-Hindus to copperplate the idol?'

Ravi was unable to control his anger at this defiance. 'Ah! Isn't that Mooshaari? The oil you use to fuel that ramshackle scooter of yours … Did you scoop that up from our local river? Don't we get oil from the Gulf?'

Achchan Namboodiri put out one more appeal. 'Anyone with a differing opinion, raise your hand.'

No hand went up. Kuttan, who had feared that his hand would go up at this juncture, had walked out earlier anyway.

So, a decision was made. The Andhithiriyan walked up to the lamp, cupped his hand, and put out the flame.

Machine Gun

'Did you figure out why the flesh was hacked off the body?' George asked Anand as they walked by the river after a visit to the mortuary.

'Haan … doesn't it make you feel that some supernatural force snuffed the life out of the body?' Anand zoomed in on the picture of the body on his phone.

George unwrapped a toffee. 'I say that was not the killer's motive. It just so happened that the act benefited him in more ways than one. I will tell you why. But first, you think for yourself. Think, think …'

Anand didn't want to overthink. He couldn't get any clue from the picture. So he put his phone away and sauntered off, admiring the flowing river. Their path lay spread out like a dead snake amidst the slush. The grass on either side was as tall as a man.

George ambled on, spreading his arms out and feeling the wild plants. The morning sun bathed the bola trees interspersed on the path, casting a golden glow on the yellow flowers. 'Lies are like these trees. If their seeds fall on any fecund spot, the saplings flourish and spread like a rash. You get the feeling that the trees are strong. The sapwood and the heartwood are all there. But the wood is brittle. It snaps easily. You can use it as firewood, but not to make furniture. A lie is also like this. It will spread in an instant, but it will not have legs to stand on. Poke at it hard enough and it will break.'

Anand rubbed his hands. 'Enough of your monologue! Get to the point. Why was the body stripped of flesh?'

'Eda, for a criminal investigation, the first thing you need is patience,' George slowed down.

'Sir, yesterday you told me that memory was the most important thing for a criminal investigation.' Anand snapped the stem off a Communist Pacha, a Siam Weed that thrived in these areas, and hurled it at George.

'Eda, the thing is, the gun we were searching for was used in this murder. The bullet was removed along with the flesh. The murderer didn't want the weapon identified. Had the bullet been found during the post-mortem, we would have cracked the case,' George said.

'Sir, are you saying that the gun we are looking for was used here? Wouldn't our case become more twisted then?' Anand sat on the rocks by the bank of the river.

'Our case was already in a tangle. If the killer sensed he was going to get caught, he would hide that gun along with his other weapons. We needed to do something before that.' George wet his feet in the river and looked at his reflection in the water. He brushed off the fish that had flocked around his legs.

'Sir, when you pull the trigger on a machine gun, don't the bullets empty out in seconds? There were four bullet wounds on the corpse. If the killer had used the machine gun, wouldn't there have been more than four wounds? Can't we examine the body once more? Not that it will lead to any proof. But why do we need to go after proof anyway? We are wasting our limited energy chasing after this. But if we find out the make of the bullet, we can be sure that the gun we are looking for is in this locality. At least our stay here would be somewhat justified.'

Anand held the low branch of a wild mango tree and joined George closer to the river.

'If the single-shot option was used, only one bullet would have been fired at a time. The killers might have had only a limited number of bullets. If that's the case, the gun would have been set to the single-shot option. All the holes in the body may not have been caused by bullets. As you said earlier, they may have excarnated the body to mimic a supernatural force to create fear. Be that as it may, I don't see the possibility of more than four rounds being fired.' George scooped up a handful of water from the river and washed his face.

A tiny anchovy slipped out of his fingers and dived deep into the river, glad for the chance to live another day.

'This one here was our first car. That Fortuner and the big cars you see there came after we made a name for ourselves. But this one, he has been with us from the start,' Pappi, a flamboyant sawmill owner, rubbed the bonnet of an old Jeep with affection. 'Sure, the paint is peeling … but a touch-up would do wonders.'

Saravanan stared at the rusty, old vehicle.

'Don't ask me why his condition is like this. This vehicle is like us. His history is a bit murky. There is a small setup below, under the chassis. I'll show you.' Pappi rolled up his sleeves. 'Look, there is a box here. You'll see it only if you lie down. In the old days, we used it to store our weapons and some colourful contraband. The key to the box is tied to the vehicle keys. You and I are the same kind of people. Which is why, I am not bargaining on the price. Come, let's sit inside. The vehicle's papers are there.'

Aadi and Pappi walked towards the sawmill, while Saravanan remained standing near the Jeep. Two months ago, he had suggested that they buy an old auto rickshaw. That conversation had gone nowhere. He had never expected they would buy a four-wheeler. The previous day, Aadi had rented a house in Purapuri, again without consulting Saravanan. They had set off immediately from Purapuri, and so, they were yet to spend a day in the new home. Before he could savour the pleasure of having a place to call his own, they were buying a Jeep.

Saravanan ran his fingers along the seat cushions. When Aadi emerged from the mill with a red file in his hand, Saravanan was already seated in the Jeep. Aadi gave the file to Saravanan and sat in the driver's seat.

'I want to live like Pappachan, at least for one day. Look at the clothes he wears! The fragrance of that perfume!' Aadi used his finger to find the ignition lock and inserted the key.

'Even you are dressed to the nines when Giri's wife comes to the temple to receive the Kodiyila.' The moment he uttered those words, Saravanan felt he had gone too far.

'The stage. Not the temple,' Aadi corrected Saravanan as he reversed the car. 'That is not because I go with the hope that they will give us the Kodiyila. But it is important to me that we clean up and go there as if we are the ones who will hold the Kodiyila that day. I want to see Giri's wife leave with the Kodiyila in her hand. Only then will the anger within me burn bright. Even now, when I saw Pappachan's black car, I thought of Giri. Have you seen this Jeep before?'

'No!' Saravanan shook his head.

'You have seen it. Perhaps your eyes were too full at that moment to see anything. But I won't forget this Jeep until the day I die. Which is why I am paying the price of gold for this scrap of metal. This vehicle is not for us to drive around. After four or five days, we are going to use it for some work. Our life's final game. I will tell you everything when it's time.'

Aadi shifted gears and backed up the Jeep.

If you drive on Eloor Bridge across the Vannathi river, you reach Ettunaad in a kilometre and a half. But the government has sealed the bridge with walls for years. So, vehicles go around in circles for twenty-six kilometres to reach Ettunaad. The route is desolate, full of emptiness and barren rocks, with no trace of grass. The only structure that stands out is the Rana Malabaricus, a palatial resort in a ghost town. The building still stands tall despite the overgrowth of weeds all around it. The government closed the Eloor Bridge and sealed access to Ettunaad after trouble erupted at the resort.

Rana Malabaricus was India's sixth-largest private resort. The resort pulled out all the stops to attract foreign tourists.

Highlights among the services and amenities offered were a three-day trek to Peelimudi and a large Theyyam performing yard constructed for three crores. About fifty residents of Ettunaad worked there. The management made sure that business flowed into neighbouring towns. They bought milk from Velarkod and Giripuram, and toddy from Pormudi. The locals helped the resort source honey and some good weed from the Peelimudi forests. The Ettunaad Council heads were willing to overlook the distorted forms of Theyyam performed at the resort. Rituals were bound to change with time, they justified. People ignored gossip about village women who made an extra buck at the resort. They believed the resort would bring progress and job opportunities to Ettunaad.

But two years ago, on 11 November, the mutual goodwill evaporated. The resort had organised various forms of Theyyam when their guests demanded it. Equations changed when the management decided to host an Irumukhan Theyyam in their performance yard. Only the local temple had staged the Irumukhan Theyyam so far, an old tradition that was not to be messed with. The village elders and a temple delegation requested the resort to cancel the performance. The resort management derided them and sent them packing. Temple authorities sent their delegates two more times. The management was firm. They even went on to erect a huge flex banner in front of the temple yard, advertising the 'performance'.

With all doors closed, the Ettunaad Council decided to act. They sent the symbolic coconut leaf and invite to their supporters. The coconut leaf, signifying a call to action, was being sent after a long interval. As part of the village's defence committee, Raghavan was brimming with pride. Recently appointed as a Nair, a leader of the temple guard, young Sreejith puffed up with joy when he saw the invite.

The performance was to be held on 11 November, a Saturday. Rana Malabaricus blazed with lights, but an eerie darkness enveloped its surroundings. The Irumukhan Theyyam was to start at 3 a.m. The guest list included international tourists and select media professionals. A popular Malayalam actor and his family added some local flavour to the mix. There were some uninvited guests too. The entire village defence committee and the temple maintenance officials turned up. They didn't come empty-handed. Scores of arrows. Twenty-four Kalari fighters. Ettillam Kannan Mooppar. An eight-membered Chaverpada, a makeshift army modelled on Malabar's famous death squads. Two sacks of swords and wooden sticks from the vaar tree. Dredging instruments. Twenty dogs. A hundred mercenaries. The Ettunaad villagers did not believe in talks or debates.

The action began in the parking lot. About twenty luxury cars were stacked up like logs and set on fire. The crack and sizzle from the fire invigorated the mob. Within five minutes, the dredging machines began breaking down the performance yard. The Kalari fighters burst into the large hall like a butcher looking for the kill in a hen coop. The alarmed guests tripped over each other as they tried to reach for the exit doors. The fighters gave them two minutes to leave, and then rolled down a barrel of diesel and threw lit crackers on it. There was a loud explosion. People scattered in all directions. The mob advanced, hitting everything in their way with iron rods. Desperate cries for help filled the corridors of that tall building.

Richard Fredrick, a German resident who had travelled from Kochi to see the Theyyam, crumbled under a wave of panic. He was suffering from PTSD. Four years ago, a bus had mowed down his girlfriend while they were walking hand in hand on the street. With only news reports to colour his perception of India, he thought he was witnessing a Naxalite uprising. The sight of blood and the murderous sounds around him made him lose control. All he wanted to do was escape. He jumped off the fourth floor into the swimming pool on the ground floor, but his bulky body missed the mark. He fell a few feet away from the pool with a thud. The sight of blood gushing out from his body removed the last sliver of humanity from Ettunaad's band of thugs. The hollers from the mob reached a fever pitch. That was only the beginning. Guests fled, leaving their bags behind as arrows flew into the crowd. Even mothers with little children were not spared in the frenzy.

Mooshaari looked at the violence unfolding around him and saw an opportunity. He had never been a hit with the ladies. He thought it was because of his physique. He fumed at this 'injustice' and hoped that one day, he would get even with the sex that had rejected him. A long time ago, he had spotted Sumathi alone. She was cutting grass on a low-lying patch of common land opposite the saline paddy fields. He tried to grab her but before he knew it, she had lacerated his lower abdomen with her sickle. Mooshaari had lost his balance and fallen. Sumathi had then pushed his head into the slush with her foot. He had stayed away from women since that day. But the hate within him grew and he was always looking for an opportunity to avenge his humiliation. Now, he felt his time had come.

His eyes fell on a slim, pretty woman. From her appearance, he guessed she was Russian. He made a vow that he would offer ten hens to Irumukhan if he got his way. He isolated the girl in a room, but she climbed down the window and ran. He had no option but to chase her. He ran past the gate of Rana Malabaricus. Past the road outside the resort. Past houses, markets and fields. He came close a few times, but she slipped out of his grasp every time.

When they reached the banks of the river, she froze. Before Mooshaari could react, she did a backflip and stood right in front of him. He was too stunned to react. She then dived down, spun around like a Catherine Wheel and kicked him in the shins. Mooshaari stumbled and fell. She removed his mundu and tied up his legs. Then, she took a rope from a boat and tied up his hands. Ignoring his screams for mercy, she threw him into the river.

The Vannathipuzha was a righteous river. Her waters had borne the schooner that carried the sacred Kshetrapalakan Theyyam, Irumukhan's trusted ally. She ensured that Mooshaari was stuffed to the gills with saltwater.

By then, the performing yard at Rana Malabaricus had turned to smoke and ashes. The resort owner, Harshavardhan Reddy, was a big fish in central politics. A few phone calls and a large police contingent was on its way to the resort. But a human chain blocked the Eloor Bridge. The CI announced on the mic that they would use force if they were not allowed to cross the bridge. The answer from the crowd came in the form of a large stone that hit the police van. The stone came close but missed the glass of the vehicle. A hail of arrows followed, piercing through the iron grills that protected the glass. This time, the glass wasn't spared. The policemen felt their weapons were as pointless as toy guns. A piece of shattered glass injured the foot of the van's driver. The CI knew that his superiors would not permit him to fire. So, he decided to make that call on his own.

But fifteen minutes before this, Reddy's eighty-five-year-old mother, who was asleep in Vijayawada, went missing. She was whisked away along with the cot she was sleeping on. The kidnappers left behind a cloth folded in a triangle, the symbol of Ettunaad, with two sticks from the vaar tree. Reddy wiped his brow.

Back at the bridge, the men stood ready for action. Before the police could pull the trigger, they were ordered to return. In exchange for Reddy's mother, the Ettunaad council demanded that he hand over the keys to the resort. And as penance, he was to offer twenty spent hens to the temple.

The cops then built a wall blocking the bridge. Four months later, the court ordered the wall to be removed. But the people of Ettunaad never used that bridge again. The residents from the eight villages were shunned. They were never considered for jobs in the neighbouring areas. Some of them were kicked out of their jobs. Even in towns far away, employers looked at them with suspicion after reading sensationalised media reports. The people of Ettunaad considered it their fate and made peace with it.

Irumukhan

Shiva's face was brighter than the crescent moon that nested on his matted locks. His luminous face lent an ethereal glow to Mount Kailash and the surrounding peaks.

Veerabhadran, who was born out of the wrath of Shiva, bowed before his Lord with utmost humility. Shiva had created Veerabhadran after the self-immolation of his consort Sati. A furious Shiva had hurled a lock of his matted hair to the ground. Veerabhadran and Bhadrakali emerged from that lock of hair.

Veerabhadran was an important part of the Bhootaganas, Shiva's band of divine companions. But even he hadn't been spared the heat of his creator's temper. He was back now at Mount Kailash after spending a year on Earth in penance.

Veera was thrilled to be back, but he was unsure if Shiva had forgiven him yet. Shiva received him with much love. Like a good host, he enquired about his well-being. Veerabhadran felt a bit relieved. He slipped in a request.

'Dear Lord, I have brought a special gift for Murugan from earth. Kindly allow me to give it to him.'

Murugan, already excited to see his beloved Veerabhadran, was now curious.

Lord Shiva raised his right hand in approval. Veerabhadran turned and called out to someone. A beautiful peacock with dense, blue feathers trailing the floor answered his call. The peacock, gleaming with a thick golden coat, walked towards Lord Shiva and sat by his feet.

'Lord, I got this creature for Murugan from Peelimudi, a forest south of Vaanikka Desham.'

Murugan was by his side before he could finish. Veerabhadran turned to Lord Shiva for approval and carefully sat Murugan on the peacock. The bird shook and rattled its train and then, much to Murugan's delight, spread out its feathers. The Bhootaganas looked on in wonder. The iridescent tawny eye spots on the peacock's golden feathers quivered in the breeze.

Veerabhadran took Murugan's spear and gently caressed the bird's neck. As if on cue, the bird swung forward. To the surprise of everyone in the room, the peacock began a beautiful dance performance. The sight of Murugan in his yellow robes and the perfect rhythm of the bird's steps brought tears to Veerabhadran's eyes.

The Bhootaganas were curious. 'Where did you bring this bird from? We haven't seen a peacock like this one before,' one of them asked.

'From a lush forest called Peelimudi in Kolathu Naadu. This peacock is not one of a kind. There are many with the same colours and beauty. But no one dances as gracefully as this one. It can also warn you when an enemy closes in,' a proud Veerabhadran explained.

Murugan felt the bird's feathers with his right hand. 'These feathers are beautiful. Your gift has made me very happy. I accept this bird as my vehicle. I will live as Payyannur Perumal in the countryside near the forest from which this beautiful mayura has come.'

Veerabhadran bowed his head in respect and turned to Lord Shiva. There was a scamper in the crowd to see Veerabhadran's next gift. But the high expectations of the crowd soon came crashing down.

Veerabhadran pulled out a slender, unremarkable plant, its desiccated leaves crumbling. He stretched out his hand to reveal a plant that looked fractured. On one side, vibrant green shoots promised vitality and impending blossoms. On the other, its withered foliage whispered of decay, dry leaves waiting to turn to dust. The poor plant looked like it was experiencing two seasons at the same time. The Bhootaganas bristled: Was Veeran insulting their Lord? At the very least, he should have gifted a pretty flower from the wild plant.

Lord Shiva wondered if Veeran was seeking vengeance because he had sent him to Earth as a punishment. His gaze bore into Veeran, ablaze with indignation. The Bhootaganas felt the temperature rise. Things were getting out of hand again. Veerabhadran tried to say something, but before he could, the wrath of Shiva that could turn anything into ashes targeted the plant. The plant burst into flames. Curly wisps of smoke melted into the air. Veeran gingerly placed the charred remains of the plant at Shiva's feet.

Shiva heard the flutter of the peacock's wings in the background and allowed young Murugan to leave. Veeran thought that was for the best. This was a plant with powers to deceive. He guessed that some in the crowd were in line for an intense experience. He was right. A few minutes after inhaling the smoke, one of the prominent Bhootaganas, Mayasu, became convinced that he was mounting a horse. He had never ridden a horse before. Mayasu found himself struggling to maintain his balance.

Samendan, who was next to Mayasu, thought he was flying through space in a chariot driven by swans. In a matter of minutes, those who had mocked that wiry plant found themselves surrendering their consciousness to it. Some in the crowd shivered out of fright. Even Lord Shiva felt his ego leave him and float slowly in a beautiful forest.

After getting off the 'horse', Mayasu's brain performed like an acrobat. Some of them in the room felt thoughts that strayed beyond their normal life of Bhakti. When the effects of the plant wore off, they felt embarrassed to be in the divine presence.

Time seemed to stand still for more than thirty minutes. Veerabhadran was nervous. But Lord Shiva's face was calm. Veeran surmised from his expression that the experience hadn't been unpleasant. He was asked a lot of questions about the intoxicating plant.

'Prabhu, this is a magical herb that grows wild in the Peelimudi forests on Earth. Soak the remaining leaves in milk and the experience will be even more intense. This is a plant that gives joy. But there is no joy left in me right now. My life on Earth was not a curse. I had this plant. If it wasn't for it, I would have suffered an unthinkable agony over not serving you for an entire year. But I wasn't anxious at all. This herb made a year seem like an hour. I feel like I cheated on my sentence. I request you to punish me again for what I did. Please sentence me again.' Veerabhadran prostrated before Shiva.

The Lord looked benevolent. 'A lot of things have happened since then, Veeran. A year has passed. You may relax now.'

'Prabhu, how can time lighten a crime? Give me a severe sentence. Please bless me.'

'Okay. Let's do what you want. Spend a year in the same Peelimudi forest but without the use of this herb. Let it be a long penance … Bhadra, what is the name of this special plant you have brought me?'

'Prabhu, I haven't been able to find out the name. Only eight families live around Peelimudi, and I haven't attempted to speak to any of them. My guess is that this plant has no name. There is no reason for it to have a name. It grows wild and doesn't seem to be of any use to anyone.'

'Is that so? Neelakandan, the blue-throated one, prefers this plant. So, let us call it Neelachadayan, meaning blue matted locks.'

One of the Bhootaganas whistled. Shiva acknowledged him with a faint smile.

Veerabhadran mixed the rest of the herb in milk and first offered it to the Lord. The crowd partook of the rest, and once more they savoured the unique Neelachadayan. Veerabhadran was still reeling from its effects when he bade farewell. A small, insignificant wild plant had made their day. Veerabhadran's heart was full when he left.

Venadhiri's estate manager, Kunjikoran, awoke to what sounded like the distant rumble of thunder. When he came to his senses, he realised it was the sound of someone banging incessantly on his door. The arrack-induced stupor from last night hadn't worn off yet. He washed his face, tried to look fresh, and opened the door. When he undid the bolt, he saw Kunki, drenched in sweat.

'You? You dog ... You are pounding on the door as if you are killing a snake. The bar of the door would have broken.' Kunjikoran was miffed that Kunki's was the first face he was seeing that day.

'Angunne ... Master ...' Kunki's tone was deferential, but was there a hint of mockery in his voice?

Kunjikoran calmed down. 'What is it, Kunki?'

Kunki was crestfallen. 'Two cows have been finished ... in the shed.'

'You hound ... When I assigned you to guard the shed, didn't I warn you a thousand times not to fall asleep?'

Kunjikoran rushed out, forgetting to wear his upper mundu. Kunki followed him to the alley, constantly apologising.

'How can I stop the tiger on my own, Thambraan?'

Kunki came up with various explanations to put himself in the clear. But Kunjikoran was in no mood to listen to excuses. 'With this attack, a total of fourteen cows have been killed. Venadhiri will crush my head today.' Kunjikoran forgot his sense of superiority for a moment and confessed his fears.

Their long walk took them across the ridges along the fields. By then, the sun was out. Kunjikoran was stunned when he entered the cowshed. The cows had been killed brutally, and their entrails were scattered across the shed. He could not stay there for long. He looked up at the eastern sky, lost in thought.

'Kunki … let's leave right away. Let's see the Master immediately. There's no other …' He rushed out before he could complete his sentence. Kunki followed him, like a cow being pulled by a rope.

From his terrace, Venadhiri saw Kunjikoran racing towards his house. He didn't spot Kunki, who was hiding by the gatehouse. Venadhiri hurried down the steps. Kunjikoran was already on his veranda by then.

Venadhiri sensed something was wrong. 'Why do you look so frightened, Kunji? What's the matter?'

'Bhagavan, the tiger has killed two more cows. The guard could not stop the tiger. The cows were killed, and their remains splattered out across four directions. Anyone would be reduced to tears at the gruesome sight,' Kunjikoran lowered his voice and gave Venadhiri a detailed account.

Venadhiri laughed. 'Of course, it will tear apart its prey. Do you expect a tiger to be genteel and lay out a sadya on a banana leaf?'

Venadhiri's heart had melted when Kunjikoran addressed him as Bhagavan, the Lord. Kunjikoran knew that word would hit the mark.

'Don't worry, Kunju. I know your supervision isn't at fault here. Let's make the cowshed stronger. We'll begin work today. There's no point delaying the work further. Can you come inside for a while?'

Kunjikoran stepped inside and caught a glimpse of Sribhadra, Venadhiri's wife. Kunji felt like the moon had descended from the sky and entered Venadhiri's bedroom. She was that beautiful.

Sribhadra took her husband behind a door. 'I know you are a fool. But do you want the whole world to know that? If we reconstruct our cowshed, won't the tiger enter the village to hunt? Won't that, too, cause you harm? Isn't it better to kill the tiger and get rid of the problem? Gather four of our best archers and lay a trap in the cowshed. They can easily finish off the tiger. And imagine all the glory and fame you'll gain!'

Venadhiri liked the idea. 'You are right. I didn't see it this way. We will go with your plan. Just do one thing: Get the kitchen to send a bowl of warm milk. Our Kunji is here … he is all exhausted and anxious.'

'In that case, you will need two bowls. Your eldest son, the cowherd Kunki, is hiding by the gatehouse.'

For a moment, Venadhiri was utterly dumbfounded. Outside, Kunjikoran heard a sharp sound, like a firecracker. After a few minutes, Venadhiri came out with an intricately carved bow and arrows.

'The wind banged the door shut. That was the sound you just heard. This is the misfortune that strikes when doors that should be shut right from the beginning are left open.' Kunjikoran hadn't mentioned the noise, but Venadhiri felt compelled to give an explanation.

'It's not wise to rebuild the cowshed. The tiger will enter the village to hunt. Laying a trap and waiting in the dark … that's the sign of a coward. We need to go to Peelimudi and kill the beast. Let Kunki himself go get his revenge. Here are the weapons you need.'

Kunjikoran's voice quivered. 'But Bhagavan …'

'What? Do *you* want to go kill the tiger instead of Kunki? Fine, then.'

Kunjikoran sensed Venadhiri's irritation. He decided not to get into further trouble. He snapped his mouth shut and collected the weapons.

Outside the gatehouse, Kunki was waiting for him, straight as a stick.

Veerabhadran had vanished, but the stories about Peelimudi still lived on in Shiva's thoughts. For once, the divine beauty around Mount Kailash failed to charm him. His mind was wavering. It is not that he didn't try to brush aside thoughts of Peelimudi. But each time, images of the jungle kept coming back to him with renewed vigour. After a while, he felt there was no point in trying to avoid a mere forest. It was always best to heed the call of the mind. The Lord decided to spend a few days in Peelimudi. That was the only way to end this craving. Of course, he could have seen every blade of grass and every grain of mud in the forest in his mind's eye, if he wanted to. But that didn't beat the joy of seeing it with the physical eye. Devi Parvathy was keen too. She wanted to see for herself the place where her son had vowed to stay.

There were many ways by which they could enter the forest. As travellers. As hunters. But the Lord felt that it was best to live in the forest as animals. So, on a cold winter dawn, Shiva and Parvathy appeared on the eastern border as a pair of tigers.

Kunki ate his last meal and set out from his hut, bent over by the weight of weapons he had no idea how to use. His wife, Naani, was lying curled up in a corner, like the dried-up tamarind pods that had fallen off the tree outside her hut. Kunki avoided looking at her.

He had barely taken a few steps when he hit the roots of a vaar tree and injured his toe. The tears streaming down his face had made it impossible for him to see what was ahead. He broke a stick from a low branch of the tree. The stick would serve as a support and help him gauge what was ahead in the forest. Also, it was the only weapon he knew how to use. He walked slowly towards Peelimudi, hoping to extend his life as much as he could.

At the edge of the forest, he felt like a sip of water. He was thirsty after the long walk in the hot sun. He saw a dilapidated hut and went in to ask for some water. The woman of the house gave him a bowl of buttermilk and asked him about his journey. She was unmoved when he told her why he was headed to the forest. But she melted when he told her about his wife, Naani, who was weeping in their house. She left the house in a hurry, instructing Kunki to wait until she returned.

She returned with seven young men from the surrounding houses. The woman had a daughter. Kunki set out with a band of eight people, including the woman's daughter.

Shiva and Parvathy were wandering across the beautiful Peelimudi, like logs adrift in the deep ocean. They took in everything with delight. From the youngest twigs to the tallest mountains spread over the forest. It wasn't even spring. But Peelimudi looked and felt like a dream. Even Veeran's high praise didn't do the place justice. They were absorbed in the beauty around them. There were tall trees that touched the sky and miles and miles of grassland. Shiva and Parvathy listened to the hum of the plants and were immersed in their surroundings. Sometimes they would forge ahead independently, their curiosity leading them in different directions. But inevitably, they would find their way back to each other and explore the lush forest together. The female tiger went to a stream on the eastern fringes of the forest and dipped her paws in the water. She relaxed in the mud. Her partner was storing away the sights in his memory as he went deeper into the forest all alone.

A few minutes inside the forest, Kunki realised it was foolish to travel with the band of helpers. They looked more like a wedding party than hunters. Forget a tiger, it looked highly unlikely that they would be able to trap even a mongoose. Kunki had seen the tiger attack the cowshed. The tiger was as fast as lightning. Kunki knew he wouldn't return alive to the village. The tiger could snuff the life out of him in the blink of an eye.

If you approached as a group, the tiger's aim might be different. The tiger might maul and kill any of these innocent villagers. Kunki thought about the possibilities and made some decisions. He gave his companions the slip and crawled towards some bushes near a large tree. As he lay still in the bushes, Kunki thought about his father, Kanitha, who would lie like a python under forest plants. Oh, the speed with which he would get up and run when he saw his Master. People said that things had changed with Venadhiri's arrival. What change? Even in his awkward position, Kunki suppressed a sarcastic chuckle. The cold bit into his bones but his mind was aflame with plots and strategies.

Kunki made sure his companions were far away and then began walking on a different route. There was a water channel thirty minutes away, which led to a stream and a round pool enclosed by stones. The locals called it Vattakulam. There was talk that the tiger was often spotted there. The villagers who came to collect honey from the forest avoided the pool. Kunki decided to head right there.

He thought about a plant in Peelimudi that turned men's brains to that of an elephant in musth. Grind the leaves in milk and drink it, and a man may sometimes lose the will to live. Kunki felt as if he had ingested that herb. Like death was pulling him towards the deep jungle by a thread. His discomfort wasn't a figment of his imagination. Even before reaching the inner forest, Kunki saw the tiger lying on a rock. The tail of the tiger was raised. That meant the beast was awake.

Kunki held his breath and stepped forward. He did not know how to aim. So, he strung five arrows into his bow. One arrow crashed beneath his foot. Some didn't travel far and fell to the ground like birds with broken wings. But one arrow hit its mark with precision. The arrow sunk into the back of the tiger's head. The tiger lay on the rock, limbs flailing.

Kunki threw away his bow and ran. He found a rock he could lift. Using all his strength, he hurled the rock at the animal. This time, too, Kunki was on target. He didn't know which part of the animal he had hit, but he heard its bones breaking, and a heart-breaking cry. Kunki felt a burst of joy.

He tried to move up the unforgiving rock. But then, he heard a faint growl behind him. He could smell danger in the air. He turned around, and a shiver ran through him. Through a cloud of dust, he saw a large tiger staring up at him. It must have been the partner of the slain tiger. He was trapped. There was a large trench of rocks ahead of him, so he could not run. His legs turned to lead.

Sometimes, death doesn't give a man any time to prepare. The tiger flung itself on Kunki and clawed at his body. In a few minutes, Kunki's body was torn apart. The tiger then climbed down the rocks and disappeared into the bushes.

Lord Shiva had wanted to take the form of an animal, and he truly transformed into one when he killed Kunki. He wandered around aimlessly after that. Only when he came to a river did he get the real picture of what had happened. His plan to live on earth for forty-one days after transferring all his powers to Virajathan seemed like a blunder now.

A tigress was relaxing by the river, her forelegs stretched out. On a nearby rock, Veerabhadran stood guard over her. The hunter he had attacked had killed an ordinary tiger, and not his Devi. Immediately, the Lord transformed back into his original form and returned to the spot where Kunki lay.

He saw an astonishing sight. The tiger's body was missing. On a rock, Kunki lay lifeless, most parts of his body burnt. Lord Shiva was unhappy. The calm exterior he had assumed as a householder began to give way to his ferocious form.

He interlocked his thumbs together and thought about Virajathan. Virajathan immediately appeared, as if he was as close as Veerabhadran was. He bowed down to his father. Without any enquiries or questions, he handed back the powers his father had entrusted him with.

When Venadhiri grew tired of his wife's curses, he sent his first-in-command Vallyedathu Nair to the forest. Nair was scouting the forest when he saw a curious sight on a rock under a huge vaar tree. A tiger lay slaughtered on the rock. Below, Kunki lay unconscious, as if he had been mauled.

Nair went closer. The tiger was dead, but Kunki was still alive. Nair hatched a plan. If the village was told that *he* had killed the tiger, he would become a hero overnight. The thought gave him goosebumps.

It had only been ten days since Nair got married. He had yet to establish his dominance in the bedroom. If news spread that he had killed a tiger, he could regain his pride. He decided to act instead of overthinking the consequences.

He took out the oil he was to use to light a torch at night and poured it on Kunki. Nair then set Kunki on fire. Kunki woke up with a scream and began crying out in pain. Nair felt a strange sensation that was very pleasurable. He poured the remaining oil to stoke the flames.

He used his tools to tie up the tiger's carcass and drag it away from the scene. By the time he returned to the village, he was bone tired. He was going to collapse any moment now. The memory of Kunki's burning flesh began to haunt him. He began vomiting so hard that he feared his intestines would spill out. He didn't want to go back home in this state. He wanted to go like a warrior, his chest puffed up, his head held high. How would he enjoy the grand welcome he was expecting otherwise?

Nair covered the tiger's body with twigs and leaves and lay down in the shade of a tree to rest.

When both Kunki and Nair didn't return, Venadhiri got worried. He had sent Nair when his wife got apprehensive after Kunki failed to return. He had told Nair to not bother looking for Kunki. 'Just roam around the jungle and have a good time.' It was past noon, and there was no sign yet of Nair.

Upon hearing approaching footsteps, Venadhiri sat up straight. He spat out the paan he had been chewing.

The footsteps climbing up the stairs were that of Narayanan, his third Vaalyakaaran, the servant who did all the hard menial work around the house.

One glance at him and Venadhiri knew something sinister had happened.

'Angunne, Vallyedathu Nair has killed the tiger.'

Narayanan repeated his sentence, but Venadhiri was still dazed.

'What? What did you say?' he screamed.

Narayanan didn't have to answer that. By then, loud celebratory sounds of 'Hoy Hoy' were getting closer to the house. Venadhiri pushed his minion aside and rushed to the terrace.

The sight he saw was joyful to him. Eight people were carrying the dead tiger on a long stick. The four legs of the tiger were tied to the stick, and its head was hanging down. Another eight people were holding up a makeshift palanquin with Nair perched on top of it. Nair was armed with a bow and arrows. His left hand was on his hip, his right hand held a sword, and his face had the pride that comes from a great victory. A cheering mob followed him.

'Bhale, bhesh ...' Venadhiri joined the chorus of the crowd.

Narayanan buttered up his boss. 'It may be the soldiers who fight, but in the eyes of the people, it's the king who is the victor. Going by that logic, it's you, Thambraan, who has captured the tiger. One word from you and your brave warriors will defeat anything, even a tiger. That's how history will remember you!'

Venadhiri raced down the steps. Nair climbed down from his perch and was standing on the highest step so that everyone could have a glimpse of him. Venadhiri enveloped him in a sweaty embrace. He removed his second mundu and wrapped it around Nair to honour him.

Nair freed himself from Venadhiri's embrace and indicated that he was eager to get home. Venadhiri ignored that request. He led Nair upstairs with a lot of show. He forced him to sit at a carved round table where a feast was laid out. Nair took a seat facing the window so that the crowd assembled outside could catch a glimpse of him. Nair ate heartily. It was a long time since he had had a good meal. Though he was enjoying the food, he was eager to meet his wife. As he ate, he began framing the story he would narrate to her.

Suddenly a deafening sound was heard. Nair was startled out of his thoughts. He first thought it was a scream. But the cheers outside were too loud for him to understand the source of the sound. He went to the window to check. He could see that people were beside themselves with excitement, but he couldn't understand why. The noise pierced his ears and he stood astonished.

Downstairs, Venadhiri struck the tiger's head again with a spear. Then, he dramatically lifted his left leg and placed it on the tiger's head. A deafening applause followed. The crowd competed to make their voices heard and raised their arms in joy.

Only one pair of hands did not go up. She was thirsting for Venadhiri's blood. She tightened her grasp on an iron rod and moved forward. Even though they guessed why she was there, the crowd looked at her with disgust. But they made way for her because they did not want to be polluted by her touch. Some thought it surreal. A woman, that too a woman like her, barging into a crowd like this!

She rushed towards Venadhiri and without wasting a moment, hurled the crowbar at him with all her might. But it was she who was hit behind her head. Venadhiri's chief estate manager had spotted an old axe in the yard, and his strong blow split her head into two. Some in the crowd heard her skull crack. The crowbar hit Venadhiri's toe. He suffered no other injury. He soon regained his composure. Then he snatched the stick that had been used to tie up the tiger's legs and began to hit Kunki's wife as if he were killing a snake. The mob was speechless for a while, but then they, too, joined their chief.

After this, Venadhiri went to take a dip in the pool. Naani's blood was splattered all over him, and he wanted to free himself from the pollution. By the time he got back, the villagers had dragged the woman's body away from the house and hung it up close to the street on three poles. From his courtyard, Venadhiri watched her body sway in the wind, while savouring a bowl of warm, sweet milk.

The crowd had thinned by then. Those remaining hung up the tiger and then headed to the pool with some oil for a bath. They wiped themselves dry in a hurry; Venadhiri had invited them back to the house for a meal.

The sight that greeted them after their bath was horrifying. Venadhiri's palatial house, which was thought to be strong enough to stand for centuries, had collapsed. Dust and debris filled the air as if an earthquake had struck. Instead of Kunki's wife's body and the tiger's carcass, two new bodies had to be hung on the poles. One of them was that of their master, Venadhiri.

4DX

Nine months ago. A Sunday

When George entered Shyamaprasad's office, the senior cop was inspecting his breakfast bowl. He was looking for a pineapple slice hidden beneath orange segments. 'My wife packs me only fruits for breakfast. She says I need to reduce my pot belly. Even if I try to grab a meal outside, she finds out. It's only a belly. Shouldn't we flaunt it instead of trying to hide it? Here … you eat this.' He pushed the plate towards George.

'No, sir … you could get used to this. People like me cannot. The government doesn't pay me enough to chop up fruits for breakfast.' George pulled up a chair with a slight smile.

'Pulling my leg so early in the day?! Ah! Leave that aside. Did you recognise the man sitting outside?' Prasad returned to chomping on his fruits.

'No, sir,' George shrugged his shoulders.

'You don't know Ashok? Ashok Senapathy?' Prasad pierced a slice of apple with his fork and looked up at George.

'First of all, I didn't see anyone outside. There's not even a baby outside. I don't know the man. I haven't heard of him.'

'Had you known him, it would have been easier.'

George savoured the look of disappointment on Shyamaprasad's face and leaned back in his chair.

'I know him, sir … I have seen his mug in the papers. I was just teasing you.'

Shyamaprasad was full of enthusiasm once more. 'Senapathy and I were batchmates at the Ezhimala Naval base. For six whole years! Senan is now a Wing Commander at Area 11, the training centre of the Air Force. He wants to meet you. He caught a flight from Kochi just to see you. That's why I asked you to come in such a hurry. I know you are busy with preparations for the weddings. But this matter is somewhat urgent.'

From Shyamaprasad's preamble, George sensed that a unique case was coming to him. He was stuck with a few dull theft cases and was beginning to get bored of his job. He hoped this would be a murder case.

Ashok Senapathy. The name instilled hope. From what he had heard so far, the man was a shark. If the great man himself had come to meet him, it could mean that his case diary was about to get interesting. But George began to wonder why such a decorated officer would seek out a cop like him.

'What is the case about, sir? Do you have any idea?'

'Idea? I have received the full script.'

Prasad pulled his chair closer. 'A baffling incident has occurred at Area 11. A woman who worked there, and a military officer on duty, went missing on the same day. At the same time. No one knows where they are. This news hasn't gone out of Area 11 yet, the outside world is not aware of this case, but it's been three months since their disappearance. Six agencies have investigated so far. No progress. These two people could not have left the campus. The four gates are heavily guarded by the Army. There is an electric fence around the property. The family of the missing woman has been told that she never entered the premises. The local police have registered a missing case.

'But the woman did enter the premises that day using her pass. The computer registered the time of entry. CCTV cameras show her entering the main gate after the security check. Until 9.17 a.m., all four cameras have an image of her. But the fifth camera does not show her leaving the premises until today.

'Twenty-six years old. Light-skinned, slim, and very tall. Okay … she is very beautiful. She is married. Normally, her husband would drop her at the gate on his bike. She took a rickshaw only if he was very busy. She would have to walk two and a half kilometres from the gate to reach her office. She is a manager at KTS, a company that has been contracted to manage transport for officers. The taxi drivers were questioned. Also, that auto driver fellow … You know Dhanesh, right? The one who runs an auto called Kanmani at the town stand. He is a young man. There are no reasons to suspect any of them because the woman had entered the premises. But they still questioned Dhanesh and all the rest of them. First in the style of our local police. After that … you know how these people behave when they feel things have gotten out of hand. They tried everything, and the case is getting more serious.'

'I mentioned the jawan who was on duty. His name is Mandal. He is from Uttar Pradesh. But he has roots in Kerala. Mandal's father, Dasan, is a Malayalee who lived in Ettunaad, a town near here in rural Malabar, a long time ago. He's dead now. They have no relatives here. We did a thorough investigation, but we haven't found a hook yet. All his details are in the file. All in all, this is a twisted case. More importantly, we are not investigating this case officially. We are not authorised to do that. Senapathy has heard about you. I thought this lady and the army officer must be in cahoots. But I can't think of any possibilities beyond that. Senapathy is under a lot of stress. He's about to retire. You can imagine the tension, right? I told him that you are one of my closest students. He has high hopes. As far as I am concerned, this is a good opportunity for you. Even though he's a close friend, I am indebted to him. I don't know if you would believe me, but I was with Senapathy when ...'

Shyamaprasad could not complete his sentence. The door opened, followed by the sound of footsteps. Even though he was curious, George didn't turn around to check. He was overcome by a sense of pride that made him hesitate. Is this that big an opportunity? From what Prasad sir said, it doesn't seem like the SIG could interfere in this case. George was immersed in his thoughts when Senapathy sat down next to him.

Senapathy smiled at him. An open, genuine smile. George had seen his passport-sized photographs in the papers a few times, but this was their first meeting. He looked ageless. A taut body that looked as if it was carved out for the forces. A pleasant expression. No one would say he was Shyamaprasad's peer. George was instantly drawn to his personality.

Shyamaprasad continued his story. 'Just before he went missing, Mandal called Watchtower 4 from his mobile phone. Manoj, a manager from Eeraattupetta, was on duty. The call lasted two minutes and eleven seconds. We are assuming that Mandal had poor connectivity. The manager said his speech wasn't clear. There was only one word that he understood: 4DX. This is the only clue we have so far. 4DX. We don't know what Mandal meant by it.'

Shyamaprasad pushed two fat files and a pen drive wrapped in plastic towards George.

Senapathy moved his chair to face George. 'Four helicopter models are placed at the first circle after the gate—we call it the Delhi circle. We had changed the wheels of one of them four months ago. The wheels came from Visakhapatnam. The batch name for these wheels was 4DX. But we haven't been able to establish any link between the wheels and this case. We don't know why Mandal mentioned that word. Like Shyam said, Mandal's phone was out of range. Also, he seemed to be in a panic as he spoke.'

'This woman you are saying went missing … what's her name?'

'Ashwini. Ashwini Radhakrishnan.' Shyamaprasad moved forward.

'Sir, Prasad sir mentioned that Ashwini wasn't spotted after crossing a particular camera. May I ask … is there any shortcut in the area behind this camera? Is there any chance she took another route?'

'No. There is no other route. There is only the main road. The traffic moves in two lanes. There are no smaller pedestrian paths. All the roads are on the map you will find on the pen drive.' Senapathy wiped his brow with a handkerchief.

'I am sorry, sir. I have a different view. A person who has to walk two and a half kilometres twice a day would surely have found a shortcut. It's human nature. If it's not too much trouble, could you cross-check that for me?'

'Sure, I will enquire about that.'

Senapathy took out his mobile phone and dialled a number. George observed his movements and expressions as he spoke to someone in Hindi.

'George, you're going to be mildly disappointed. There is no such shortcut there. I told you, right? The layout doesn't allow for such alternative routes. But I like the way you think!' Senapathy put his phone on the table.

'Thank you! What age would this Mandal be? He is a man past middle age, right?'

Shyamaprasad butted in. 'No, Mandal is young. He is twenty-six.'

'Oh? But isn't it the DCC who handles security?'

Shyamaprasad didn't know the answer to that one.

'Yes, George, that's how it works normally,' Senapathy said. 'But recently, we had a call from Delhi about a bomb threat. So, we were directly handling security.'

George was about to ask his next question but a phone call interrupted them. This time, Senapathy spoke in a language that sounded close to Hindi but wasn't Hindi. Senapathy's poker face hid his emotions. But George could make out that he was getting some unexpected news.

'George, your guess was correct. There is an alley there that I don't know about. At first, they told me there weren't any other routes. But when the guards asked people who commute every day, they found one. It's a small pedestrian path that takes you from the main road to the fire station. The beginning of the path is strewn with weeds. That's why I didn't notice it. The path is a few feet away from the circle where the helicopters are displayed. Would Mandal have made that call because something strange happened on this path?'

Senapathy was breaking into a sweat.

'There's nothing to suggest that an ordinary jawan like Mandal knew that the wheels belonged to the 4DX batch. For argument's sake, let's assume he did. Say he saw something and wanted to describe it. Any of us would mention 'helicopter'. Why would we speak about the wheels? Unless it came up as part of a specific conversation. Hanging on to the word 4DX may not get us anywhere. We may need to look at the possibility that your investigation has begun with a few false premises. The fact that your team did not know about the alley is a big loophole. For this reason alone, I feel it wouldn't be wrong if I took a shot at this case. I am not confirming if I will, but l will try to. That's all. Don't consider it insubordination if I ask you something else. During your phone call, did you instruct your team to clear the mouth of that path?'

'Yes, I have asked them to do that.' Senapathy seemed relieved that George was getting involved.

'Sir, can you leave that spot as it currently is until I have taken a look? Can you ask them not to alter anything on the scene for now?'

Senapathy agreed. He had already been told of George's style. He delved deep into things.

No one spoke for a while. For the first time since George had walked in, the room was quiet. Senapathy looked around the room. He had never been to Shyam's office before. The room reflected Shyam's innate sense of order and discipline. Not even a paper was out of place. He was admiring the decor when Shyamaprasad turned to him again.

'George spoke about basic human nature. I've been thinking since then about man's other basic instincts: love and romance. Mandal is an army man. That doesn't make him immune to the charms of love. After all, you fell in love and got married while you were an officer. Mandal and that woman are human after all. What if they have run away together? I know security is tight in the campus. But what if Mandal's familiarity with the area helped him create a plan to bypass the security? What do you think?'

Senapathy, who had his eye fixed on a bookshelf, didn't flinch. 'That's laughable. An elopement couldn't happen. Even astrologers who use a parrot to pick a card to foretell the future wouldn't come up with such a dramatic story.'

'When you say something like this could never happen, you've made a pre-judgement. Pre-judgement won't get us anywhere in a case. What do you say, George?'

'Sir, I have only read two pages of the file so far. If the facts recorded here are correct, there is no chance that your theory is correct. Because along with Mandal, a gun went missing. Mandal would well be aware of the repercussions of a military gun going missing. It's unlikely he made off with a gun as part of a plan to be with his lover ...' George stopped. He was uncomfortable defying his senior in front of an outsider.

'You are right. When he went missing, Mandal had a light machine gun on him. We have lost no less than thirty bullets. That makes the case even more serious. I am in a soup. I request you, George, to help me. I am willing to pay you for the time you spend on this case. And I will provide any resources you need.'

The senior officer's plea didn't go down well with George. He felt a disciplined officer wouldn't let his emotions get the better of him.

'I know we can't investigate this officially. If Shyam sir and you insist, I will go on leave immediately. I need to be paid an amount equal to my regular salary for the days I am on leave. I don't need a rupee more. I will do my best. I cannot promise you anything else as of now.'

Senapathy instantly agreed. George opened his laptop bag and packed the files and the pen drive. He walked out of the room and took out some chewing gum from his pocket. When he came closer to his car, he realised he had left the keys behind. He went back to Shyamaprasad's room. At the door, he heard Prasad sing his praises to Senapathy. He felt embarrassed to knock, and decided to ditch his car and take the bus.

Freed from the distractions of driving, George used the bus journey to reflect on the case. There was no shred of evidence. Unlike his earlier investigations, he had no hints or suggestions he could go by. He wasn't even sure of the exact nature of the crime he was investigating. All he had in front of him was a word isolated from a conversation: 4DX.

Back home, George was in the middle of cooking dinner. He was on a restricted diet after a diagnosis of haemorrhoids. He was mostly vegetarian and ate eggs only on Sundays. Meat was a rare indulgence, reserved only for the most demanding days: days of long interrogations, gruelling prison rounds, or late-night dinners with his superiors.

He had just chopped onions for an omelette when he heard a horn at the gate. He switched off the stove and stepped out. The gate was open, and the car was already on the porch.

'Anand … Doing great, I hope!'

Anand, who was trying to extricate the tangled handle of a bag from the boot, stuck his head out.

'Sir, how did you know it's me? I had my face buried in here.'

He continued his struggle to get the bag out.

'Shyam sir said you were coming.' George gently pushed Anand to the right and tugged at the bag. One pull to the left, and the bag was out. 'There's a hook inside that knots the bag. I had got it installed for another reason.' He checked that the bag wasn't damaged before handing it over to Anand.

'Anand, son … have you heard of 4DX?' George asked Anand on their way to the kitchen.

'No. I've heard of RDX. It's a chemical used for explosions.'

'Oh really?! This is the first time I'm hearing of it.'

Even though George's tone was serious, Anand knew he was pulling his leg. Anand liked this camaraderie. George never flared up at him or gave him the silent treatment. He wondered why despite having an army of proteges and juniors, George always preferred to take him, a driver, along. Working with George sir was like going on a vacation to your hometown. He was never irritable or irritating. Apart from the rare times he behaved like a crazy man, he was quite okay. If Anand lay low on those days, it was a fun experience. Compared to working with Shyamaprasad or Arun sir, the days with George sir were like a holiday.

'Sir, when you make an omelette, it's best to beat the yolk and the egg white separately. Mix it in the end and whisk again. That's the secret of a good omelette. Move aside. Let me make it for you.' Anand took control of the kitchen.

George picked a handful of raw onions to munch on. 'How come you're such a good cook, Anand? I am not trying to flatter you, but everything you cook is so delicious.'

'Sir, I was a driver on packaged tours for a long time. When I travelled with groups of college students, I had to cook hot meals for them. That's how I began cooking. Also, men who rarely enter the kitchen are usually very good cooks. When you don't have to do something as a daily chore, and you're doing it for pleasure, you are enjoying the process.' Anand swirled the pan to spread the oil.

'May I ask you a question I swore never to ask? When our Janathan sir and Haridas are all available, why do you always choose me to travel with you on cases? I am only a driver. On second thoughts, I can't even call myself a driver. I am not very good at driving. Everyone who has met me dismisses me as a beggar, a good-for-nothing. Even my family doesn't respect me all that much. But you always seek me out when you are on a case. What's the deal?'

'Are you finding it tiresome to come along with me?' George took out two beer bottles from the fridge.

'Ayyo, sir ... no. I am asking you because there is no trouble at all. If you tell me what it is about me that you appreciate, I will try to keep doing what I am good at.' Anand lowered the heat on the stove.

'As you say, Janathan and the rest have proved their mettle by solving cases. I admire their capabilities, and perhaps that's why I never seek their help during a case. We never hire two chefs for a wedding sadya, do we? If two genius chefs get together to make one curry, I can guarantee you it will be tasteless. What an investigator needs is not another investigator, but a companion. I think you are very street smart.'

'Have you ever been to the Air Force's Area 11?' George handed over a beer mug to Anand. Anand would have preferred drinking out of a bottle, but he took the mug George offered him.

'I haven't been inside. But back when the strike was on, I had gone up to the gate.'

'Strike? What strike?'

'It's not a recent event. It happened many years ago. When the government took over that land for Area 11, this region lost a temple that was inside the premises. There was a strike then, where we demanded the right to worship in that temple. My grandfather was part of the strike. He wasn't strong enough to travel alone for a long distance. So, I went along. A long time ago, people came to that temple after buying bulls, buffaloes and oxen from the famous Subramanya cattle fair in Karnataka. The cattle were made to travel on foot. They would first be brought to this temple before they were taken home. The deity was Nairaneeshwaran. A very powerful god. A form of Siva. My mother used to say that I had accompanied my grandfather to the temple. I don't remember that. In those days, a prize ox would fetch two hundred rupees. Today, you wouldn't even get a plate of beef for that.'

Anand downed his beer and sprinkled chopped onions on the egg.

'The strike did no good. They never let us inside. We were protesting outside, but we didn't know if the temple was still intact or if it had been demolished.'

George liked listening to stories from the past over a drink.

'After ten or fifteen days, the strike ended on its own. We were sweating outside, but they were firm about not letting us in. There are radars there. Very tight security. Turns out they didn't demolish the temple. I am told it's still there. But they worship a different god. Jagannath. I hear they have a Hindi pujari. None of us know where Nairaneeshwaran is. The curse of that act still lingers there. Didn't you read the papers last month? A group of kids who were being trained there drowned in the sea. Got to be careful when you mess with the gods.'

Anand gulped down his beer.

That night, Anand lay on his stomach, trying to catch some sleep. His thoughts were full of Area 11. A flat, wide expanse of land below twelve hills. The superstitions that once shadowed the area came rushing back to him. He remembered the folklore about the Nairaneeshwaran temple and the names that had crept into his mother's bedtime Yakshi stories. Ever since the Central Government took over, people began to say the infrastructure was on par with developed nations. Anand had never gone back after the strike. When George said Area 11 was to be their first stop tomorrow, Anand got excited. Even though he didn't know the details of the case, he could sense that this time, George had a whale of a puzzle to crack.

Anand needed a break from the unpleasant memories that had been haunting him for the last two months. Until his eyes closed from sheer exhaustion, Area 11 dominated his thoughts. The name itself was a vehicle that would take him to his past.

Anand woke up late the next day. When he finished his morning chores and rushed outside, George was washing an old tipper truck. The plastic trays of the tipper looked like the ones used in fish trucks and were strewn all over the yard. Anand kicked one out of curiosity and the stench of rotting fish and garbage spread through the air. It made him retch.

He swallowed in disgust and walked towards George. 'What's all this about, sir?'

George brushed him aside, asking him to get dressed quickly. It was already past 8 by then.

Anand rushed inside for a shower. Even before he was out, he could hear the honking from the yard. He grabbed the first T-shirt he saw and sped out. George was waiting for him. He seemed to have transformed into a new person. He was wearing a faded Argentina football team jersey and a saffron lungi. Anand was used to George's ways, so he wasn't completely taken aback. If George set out to do something, he would persist until he reached the end of it.

The tipper was an old one. Looks like it was made when the wheel was invented, Anand thought wryly. As they made their bumpy ride to Area 11, he felt as if he were trapped in a washing machine. He was relieved when the journey was over.

Even though Senapathy had informed the security office in advance, they had to wait in a queue for an hour and a half. After some more painful protocol checks, the King

Cobra finally gave them a pass to enter the premises for a day. Senapathy had playfully nicknamed the security officer King Cobra. The man spent his entire shift cooped up in a glass booth like a prized exhibit at the Snake Park.

George was patient while waiting in the queue. But he began to lose his cool when the security camera couldn't get a picture of him even after twenty attempts. After the photo, there was another long wait for Senapathy's man, Anthony, who was to show them around. When the heat became unbearable in the cubicle, Anand and George stepped out. Outside, there was an interlock-paved yard that was the size of a bus stand. The yard was dotted with tents. From a distance, it looked like a circus troupe was in the area. Beyond the yard was a four-lane road that would take them to Area 11. About three kilometres away was a huge arched gateway, constructed in the traditional Kerala Padippura style. About ten armed men manned both sides of the gateway. Each vehicle was stopped and its occupants had to step out for a body search. Four armed soldiers were stationed on top of the gateway for an aerial view of the vehicles.

Opposite the tent was a building whose facade looked like the ticket station of a movie hall. Visitors had to enter their pass number and phone number to enter. Those with a permanent pass could flash their ID in front of a computer. A large screen above displayed their photograph, employment details, and the time of entry. They had to wait in a small queue to pass their bags through the metal detector.

But the queue for temporary passes seemed neverending. The queue mostly comprised workers from other states and older women in green uniforms. The thought of standing behind all of them for another long wait made Anand's head spin.

After about twenty minutes, Anthony finally made an appearance. He looked like a copy of Senapathy: a handsome, fit young man. He apologised for being late. Within two minutes, they got their passes.

'You see that small building over there? It looks like a Milma milk booth. Show this pass there. They will give you a number. Write it down or memorise it. Don't worry. You can go straight in. You don't have to stand in the queue. I will ask Saab to call them right away.'

Anand was relieved. Things moved at lightning speed after that. Anand and George wrote down their pass numbers—361 and 360—on their hands and walked towards Anthony. He asked them to get the truck.

Security was smooth because they had Anthony with them. Anand felt that their rickety vehicle was a little less bumpy now because of the smooth roads. He cursed under his breath as a bus overtook them.

'There's a bus service within the campus?' Anand asked Anthony.

'A bus in the morning, and another in the evening. They are buses that come from outside and pass through the campus.' Anthony, who was squeezed into the passenger seat next to Anand, adjusted his position.

'Isn't that a big risk?' Anand asked. 'How would you know who's on the bus? If even one passenger can slip out, what's the use of your much-celebrated security measures?'

'The bus passes by only in the morning and evening. From the gate that we just passed through, three DCC men get into the bus. They stand at the door. If anyone wants to exit the bus, they have to show their passes to these DCC men. Until the bus reaches Kozhikode Gate, the officers stand guard at the door.'

Anthony showed Anand the way, pointing to the left.

'Oh … so, do these buses go to Kozhikode?' Anand steered to the left and got on to a narrow road.

'No, Anand. Kozhikode Gate is the name of a gate that is about fourteen kilometres from here. The bus goes to Payyannur.'

Anand was surprised that Anthony called him by his name. The road they were travelling on was narrow, with large football fields on either side. He counted at least thirty-five courts. Anand hoped that if ever the soccer World Cup came to India, it would happen here.

They stopped in front of the first house on the street. Anand followed George with a tray from the truck, but he had no idea why they were there. George stopped at a garbage bin behind the garage of the house. He began scooping the contents of the bin into the tray. The mystery of the trays was finally solved. They went to four more houses in a row, and Anand felt compelled to help George.

The bins hadn't been emptied for at least three days. Anand retched as he handled the unsegregated waste. Kitchen waste, plastic, remnants of curries, rotting fish … In some houses, diapers and used condoms were mixed with the kitchen waste. When they loaded the trays and made their next stop, the work they had done so far seemed like a breeze.

The dumping yard stretched out like a mountain of garbage in front of them. The painstaking task of segregating waste for the entire property was done here. Curries leaking fluid, food crawling with worms, rotting carcasses of roadkill—everything was part of that giant, stinking heap. A stench that made you think your lungs would explode. Several workers, including two older women, were hard at work. Anand kept his distance, but George helped with the unloading, and soon, toiled among the workers as if he was one of them.

Anand was sure the stench wouldn't bother George. The most unpleasant smell in the world is that of rotting human flesh. George always showed a keen interest in post-mortems. He wasn't particularly repulsed by the dumping yard of Area 11 and its surroundings.

After unloading all the trays, George had a nice, long bath. He was marking out the day's stops and routes on a chart when he noticed Anand sitting glumly by the washing stone in the yard. Anand was lost in thought. He didn't hear George's footsteps behind him.

'What happened? Is the work getting too hard? Didn't I tell you not to join us in gathering waste? All you need to do is drive the tipper.' George opened a tap nearby to wash his feet.

'The work is not a problem, sir. We have done so much worse. I was thinking about the situation back home. Our house has been demolished. I hoped to rebuild it immediately. The loan amount wasn't enough. I used some of that money to repay some old debts. When it began to drizzle now, I got a bit nervous.'

'Don't worry about all that now. If it's money you need, I have more than enough right now. Last month, I cashed five lakh rupees from a chit fund. What do I need all this money for? I saw you looking up at the sky. I was wondering what magic show was being played up there. That's why I came out to check on you.'

As George spoke, dark clouds parted to reveal a half-formed moon. Anand lost himself in the celestial beauty, forgetting his worldly troubles for a while.

Over the next two days, they used Anthony's absence as an excuse to venture deeper into Area 11. They pretended to be lost. The flat land among eleven hills, well hidden from public view, was about a hundred times bigger than what they had imagined it to be. Within two days, Anand realised the futility of looking for clues in this vast expanse of land. It was like searching for a fish that had slipped away from your palm into the ocean. But George's enthusiasm increased by the day.

On the third day, they conducted a thorough search in the alleyway near the helicopter display. This was where Ashwini had last been seen. Grass as tall as a man hid the alley from the bustle of Area 11. Deeper inside was a long-abandoned workers' colony. Creepers and trees had taken over the five hundred-odd houses in the colony. Many of the structures had been destroyed by time and nature. The area looked like a village abandoned in the middle of a forest. You could bury a man here and no one would know. When you walked further, you reached the dumping yard, where there were at least some signs of activity. The road after the yard was not tarred, but it was sufficiently wide. This road was always abuzz with tippers, trucks and excavators making their way to the dumping yard.

But the area between the dumping yard and the helicopter display ran wild. The terrain was so different that it seemed like a dense forest. Every other part of Area 11 was well planned but here, everything grew wild, and even the manmade structures were overrun by nature.

After five days of exploring Area 11, George identified three vulnerable points along the property's perimeter wall. These were spots from where someone could potentially escape undetected.

Two of these spots were at least sixteen and twenty kilometres away from the alley. One of them was a stream that flowed into Area 11. There were bars built within the wall to let the water flow in but, with time, the bars had become rusty and broken. If the water level was low enough, a man could easily slip in or out. Beyond the stream was an old abandoned ancestral house. The wilderness outside hid the house, and any possible activity there. Four kilometres beyond that stood a large tree with branches that spread well beyond the property. When you looked at the tree from inside the property, much of it seemed hidden by a large building of the Kerala State Electricity Board that was no longer in use. Outside the wall was an autorickshaw stand and a busy market. It would be hard for anyone to escape undetected during the day or to use these two routes to slip out of the property. If not the eyes of people, the cameras would spot them. These factors led to the possibility of a third way out.

The likelihood of the third route being used was higher because it was closest to the alley. In the thick wilderness, a distinct high, squarish hole had been carved into the wall above which ran an ordinary electric line.

Anand inspected the hole in the slippery, moss-covered wall, which had been overrun by plants. 'Sir, let's consider for a moment that the commando slipped out through this opening. I doubt a civilian woman could manage that.'

'He might have helped her. Besides, a woman can do whatever a man can. They were both human beings,' George replied. George used a rope to climb up the wall. He slid out of the hole and reached outside the boundary. Anand followed him, struggling. As he emerged, Anand realised they were now on higher ground. From inside, the hole had appeared to be at a considerable height, but from outside, it looked like a depression below ground level.

'This crevice hasn't been opened recently. At least two or three monsoons have rained down on this cavity. If they went out this way, there must have been some extraordinary reason for Mandal to lead her through this route. If that was the case, Mandal's gun and uniform would still be somewhere in this wilderness. If we don't find the gun here, there could be two reasons. Mandal might have had a detailed strategy chalked up in advance to get out of here. That seems unlikely though. Or, it is possible that they were killed within the property.'

George fished out his mobile and took pictures of the breach in the wall from various angles.

'I don't buy what you're saying … that the two of them made a plan and gave the slip. I don't think an officer on duty would elope with a girl. Maybe he killed her and escaped through this breach.'

George evaluated Anand's theory for a second while continuing to take pictures.

'Mandal may have killed her. But then, he wouldn't try to escape. A murder happens and he goes missing the same day. Wouldn't he be the obvious suspect even if someone else committed the crime? But there's another side to what you're saying, Anand. Let's continue to presume that Ashwini was murdered. Let's look at this another way. Imagine you, Anand, killed Ashwini. Now, picture Mandal passing by and witnessing the act. Mandal had the authority and strength to overpower you in a minute. How would you have reacted in such a situation? You would have killed Mandal. That would have been your only option if you wanted to save yourself from the noose, right?'

'Yes, under regular circumstances, sir. But when Mandal went missing, he had a gun with him. A machine gun. Now, do you think anyone would put up a fight?'

This wasn't an unexpected question. George said, 'That would work if the murderer was an ordinary person like you. What if the opponent was also armed with an equally powerful weapon? It would be akin to two nuclear-armed nations facing off. A gun would not have any relevance there. It would have come down to a fistfight.'

Anand felt George's line of thinking was logical, but he had a doubt. He didn't have time to voice it for George had climbed back into Area 11 through the breach. Anand wondered if the question he wanted to ask was silly. It probably was.

They poked around the dumping yard until evening. It wasn't all that bad. In the evening, George came up with a plan that terrified Anand. George wanted to spend the night in one of the houses in the colony abandoned by workers. Even during the day, an eerie atmosphere hung around the colony. Anand couldn't fathom the horror of being in the area after dark. But he thought it would be inappropriate to tell George about his fears, so he kept mum. When George had offered to pay the money required to build his house, Anand's respect for him had only grown. Of course, Anand would never accept the money. But the conversation surely gave him a lot of hope and lifted his spirits. Anand felt obliged not to stand in the way of George's decisions when it came to work.

That night was more frightening than Anand had imagined. A slight gust of wind would stir up the wilderness with a roar. The howling of foxes as they came too close destroyed any shred of courage Anand had. He found comfort only when Anthony dropped by with a chicken.

Anand marinated the chicken with spices and began to skewer the pieces on a metal wire.

'A long time ago, when my younger brother was born, my father and I were on our way to the hospital on his bicycle. A snake appeared right in front of us and our bicycle overturned. As I struggled to escape, the snake crawled over and twined itself around my legs. I have never been more scared in my life. Since that day, I have been mortally afraid of snakes. I think of that and even today, a cold, uncomfortable sensation slithers up my body. I have always avoided wild places like this ever since that incident. But today, I got trapped here …'

Anthony had gathered some firewood and was stacking them up.

'They say there is a python somewhere out here. A gigantic, reticulated python. A large and long snake as thick as an elephant's thighs. Many have spotted it in the dumping yard.'

Anand had expected some comforting words from Anthony. This new information was like a slap on his face.

'Why Anthony … why is this place alone overtaken by the forest? Isn't this too a part of Area 11?'

'This land is all ours. True. Do you see this trivet we have created to roast the chicken? That's the answer to your question. This is no ordinary branch. It's called the Vaar Vadi. There is a temple inside here. Many devotees once thronged this temple. Worship and puja are still offered to the god. The young branches of this specific tree are used in many rituals associated with that deity. The god here had a favourite Theyyam, a Theyyam that was once attacked and eaten by a tiger. The Theyyam was then tied to this tree's branch and brought to the village. An aunt, a friend of my Mamma, told me these stories. Anyway, the rule is that the young branches of this tree can be stripped only for the rituals of that temple. If you chop off the young branches for any other reason, the prevalent belief here is that you will die in forty-one days. We are now using the dried-up branches that have fallen off the tree naturally. The young ones should not be touched. That is why the forest has been allowed to remain here as it is. Even though these people swear by modern military rigour, they are deeply superstitious. In one sense, you can't blame them. Who wants to toy with the heavens?'

Anthony took the skewered chicken from Anand and walked towards the fire.

'Sir, so did our Mandal die after chopping off a Vaar Vadi?' Anand sat cross-legged by the bonfire, ready to hear more stories.

George moved a few twigs closer to the fire with a stick. 'Anand, we may be sitting around a fire, but we are cops, not sorcerers. Don't think irrationally.' Flames leapt up and covered the chicken carcass and tiny embers scattered into the air in the cool breeze.

Anand stared at the chicken, which was beginning to turn brown. 'In my father's time, we would only get chicken curry after the hen became a spent hen. No one would roast or fry the chicken then. The chicken would be curried and eaten with dry, white rice. Today, eating chicken is as common as drinking lime juice. Everything changes with time, including the way we approach relationships.'

Anthony was curious. He moved closer and looked at Anand's face glowing in the flames. 'Actually, where are you from, Chetta? What is this spent hen?'

'A long time ago, we lived in Kerala, here in Malabar. Then we moved to Tamil Nadu after my father died. My mother is from Shakti Nagar, near Erode. When I grew older, and the situation improved, I came back here to complete my studies. We couldn't quite feel settled there. This is our soil, after all. Spent hen or Chandi Kozhi is no complex thing. Don't we rear hens for eggs? After the hen stops laying eggs, it's considered Chandi, which means waste, or a spent hen. Exactly what we do to human beings. When people are of use, we proudly flaunt them before the world. After we grow weak, we all turn into Chandi Kozhi … you, me, sir … everyone.' Anand's voice melted into the night air.

The sky lit up with a million stars, but the three of them were transfixed by the tiny sparks of light flying from the fire. George wanted to sneak in a few questions during this friendly conversation. But since Anthony and Anand were talking non-stop, he couldn't get a word in. They were closer to each other in age, and there was no dearth of topics. George didn't get a chance to butt in as they chattered on, laughing and joking. When the chicken was almost done, the atmosphere quietened a little. It was one of George's no-chicken days. Anand wasn't fond of a roast either. In short, Anthony found himself in a large boat with a single oar. A light eater, he sweated in front of that whole chicken.

George seized the opportunity. 'Anthony, have you heard of 4DX?'

'Yes, I have.' Anthony's cryptic answer put George in a spot. Anand and George had to wait for Anthony to chew a large piece of chicken before they got the rest of the answer.

'4DX? It's the name of a movie hall in town. I've been there once. It's a small theatre. Just about thirty seats.' Anthony reached out for another piece of chicken, but George pulled the plate away.

'Only thirty seats?' Anand asked.

'Yes, you know 3D films, right? This theatre screens 4D films. We experience smells and heat as we watch the movie. You dress well for a show, and sometimes you find drops of water on your clothes and face. It's annoying. And one ticket costs 300 bucks! Don't even think of wasting time there.'

George savoured the nicely roasted chicken with his eyes. 'Why is this place called Area 11? Some say it is because the property is surrounded by eleven hills. Is that true? Or is it some code that the Air Force uses?'

'Yes, it has been named so after the hills. But, sir, these are no ordinary hills.' Anthony lowered his voice. 'Two of these hills are said to be Soorpanakha's breasts. Remember how Rama chopped off her breasts and hurled them into the air? The breasts landed here. There are two hills named after her breasts here. Even when Area 11 was being created, those hills were left untouched. There's not even a watch tower there.

The highest point here is in one of those hills. If you stand at the summit of that hill, you can see the entire district.' Anthony was miffed that it was dark, and he could not point out the hills to George.

'There are strange beliefs here, right?' It was the first time George had heard about the Soorpanakha hills.

'Oh, this is nothing. About thirty kilometres from here, there is a region called Ettunaad. Like how we roasted this chicken over a fire, they roast human beings alive over fire. When we first came here, Mamma said she wanted to see a Theyyam and so we went to Ettunaad. Mamma almost fainted. Everyone there is a bit off. Everybody in Ettunaad is crazy.'

'Ettunaad? Where have I heard that name before?' George jogged his memory. 'Right! The hometown of the late Mandal!' He turned to Anthony.

'Theyyam reminds me … you said there is a temple inside Area 11. But is there a Theyyam here? Outside in the market, there are three Theyyam shrines.' George had been wondering about this ever since he first stepped into Area 11.

'There is a ruined temple. Bali is the Theyyam there. After being slain by Rama's arrow, Bali lives on here as a Theyyam. The story goes that the Theyyam came here with a local carpenter who had gone to Hampi for some work. The Theyyam's name is Nedubaliyan, I think. Like us humans, Theyyams also love to travel. Many of the so-called villains of the Ramayana live here, in some form or the other.'

Anthony was full now. Anand looked at him sitting disinterestedly before the food and thought about a lone cop protecting a corpse. Memories began to stir, and he got uncomfortable. The ability of men to travel back in time through memories is a curse. Anand looked up at the sky and tried to distract himself with other thoughts.

By then, George had fallen asleep, still seated. The heat and the intense search of the day had worn him out. His snores were louder than usual and pierced Anand's ears. Anand flitted from thought to thought and finally drifted into a deep slumber.

When Anand woke up, George and Anthony had already resumed their search in the dumping yard. They were being assisted by Sahadevan, a worker in the yard. Anand had slept in fits and starts. First, there was the buzz of mosquitoes that had swarmed his sheet, trying to get in. Then, he had heard strange sounds and the cries of animals he never knew existed. He felt like he was in the middle of a storm. Nature behaved as if she had made a deal with fear that night.

In the yard, Sahadevan was looking at a small hill of beer bottles with regret. 'These heaped-up beer bottles alone would fetch us enough tea money for a week. But here, they don't let us sell these bottles. They don't eat and they don't let us eat! But sometimes, we sneak out a bottle or two. The money we earn working at the dumping yard is hardly enough to buy cooking gas for our homes.'

George, who was sorting out the unbroken bottles, caught on. 'How do you manage to sneak out stuff from here?'

'Oh no, sir … it's not that we steal anything. After training, the young officers leave behind a lot of junk. They don't carry the stuff back home. They can buy anything from the canteen at three quarter the price. So they are okay with dumping stuff here. New clothes, tables, home theatre systems and bicycles … everything lands up in the dumping yard. Even washing machines. All branded. We can spend a lifetime picking trash and yet we would not be able to afford to buy this stuff. How can we let these things rot in a ditch? When we spot something we want, we tell Satyajit … he is an operator at the dumping yard. He uses his JCB to lift the goods and put them among the bushes over this wall. We don't do it often. People like us can never save enough money to buy these things. Our lives run in reverse gear.' Sahadevan became aware of Anthony's presence and stopped.

Anthony was chewing on a wild leaf, listening with interest. 'Isn't there this guy from Kollam, Abdullah? Doesn't he have a contract to collect all usable waste?'

'He only takes iron and cardboard. He is not interested in electronic goods. I told you right at the beginning, no? We have only taken one or two things. Used stuff that no one wants. We haven't burgled anything.' Sahadevan cursed himself for having spoken too much.

George was careful to choose the right words. 'So, if anyone needed to take something out of here … Satyajit is the man to go to? Isn't this Satyajit the one who was accused of assaulting a woman? There's a case going on … isn't that so, Anand?'

'Ayyo, sir! There's no way it can be Satyajit. You must be talking about his cleaner. A fellow named Akhil. He is a weird guy. Behaves strangely in front of women. Satyan is a meek fellow. He helps us out because he knows our situation. He's no accessory to theft.'

Sahadevan was the perfect bait. George gave Anand a slight smile. Through the day, he asked Sahadevan seemingly innocent questions. But the day's search was a failure. There was no clue to latch on to even the next day. George decided to expand his search outside Area 11. He planned to visit Ashwini's folks and the premises of 4DX theatre.

They finally left Area 11. For the first time in three days, Anand slept soundly, secure within the four walls of George's home. The cool breeze of the fan and a closed room seemed more precious than drinking water to him. He woke up early to fix breakfast and do some chores. George wanted to leave for 4DX at 11 a.m., but all his plans went awry. The car wouldn't start. Anand tried all the tricks he knew. Strange sounds emanated, but the car was in no mood to cooperate. Anand opened the bonnet and tried to figure out what was wrong. That took an hour.

Anand was sweating profusely, and he decided to take the battery out. 'There's no point trying further, sir. I will remove the battery and get it charged outside. The car hasn't been used for a week. Maybe the battery has drained. If it still doesn't get charged, I will look for an electrician.'

George was on the veranda, enjoying a cup of tea. 'In that case, can't we push the car to get it started? Won't a running vehicle charge the battery automatically?'

'That doesn't work on new cars, sir.' Anand removed the battery and placed it on a scooter.

George had got dressed early and was already tired of the long wait. So, he too stepped out with Anand. George had moved into town only a short while ago. Few people knew who he was. But they got a few friendly waves and nods along the way.

Anand took George to a spare parts shop across from South Indian Bank. The store gave customers a spare battery while theirs was being charged. Unfortunately, the employee in charge of batteries was on a lunch break. The store owner was deferential to George because he was a cop, but they had to wait until the employee came back from his long lunch break. George began to observe the drivers who came in with their crumpled clothes. He paid attention to the diverse tools and parts they asked for.

The universe conspired to turn things around that day. A stranger who walked in attracted George's attention. His appearance and manner were ordinary. But he did something unusual the minute he walked in. He took out a packet of snuff from his pocket, spread some on his palm and pressed it with his thumb. He then went to the yard where there was a flock of pigeons and scattered some snuff around. He watched the pigeons eat with a smug, satisfied expression. Apart from Anand and George, no one else seemed to take much notice of him. He locked eyes with them a few times.

The man had worn his mundu high up as if he had come wading through a flood. He unfolded his mundu and walked up to the counter. 'Chetta … one 3DX accelerator cable. Only inner.'

After he had bought the cable, he turned around to look at George one more time. George nodded at him. In response, the man flashed a pleasant smile that George would remember for a long time. He waited in his chair for a while after the man had left and then walked up to the counter.

'Chetta … one 4DX accelerator cable. Only the inner.'

Anand stood up from his chair when he heard George.

'We don't store parts of the 4DX. We only deal with 3DX parts. Check with the company, they will be able to help you.'

Both Anand and George were shocked. They had taken a stab in the dark and somehow hit their mark.

'Why don't you store parts of the 4DX here?'

The salesman was annoyed. He wanted to be rude, but he had noticed how Anand had constantly referred to George as sir. He was convinced that George was a high-ranking officer. So, his reply was restrained,

'No one would buy it from us, sir. There are only a couple of 4DX in this region. 3DX parts move very fast because everyone uses them. That's why we deal in them.'

'So, only two people have 4DX here. Who are those people?'

'One of them is with a construction firm, LK Group. They do all the road work in this region. Only they can afford it. It's very hard to operate. The other is an Ernakulam vehicle. It runs within Area 11 on a contract.'

'Area 11, is it?' George made a fist and struck the table. The tabletop was glass, but luckily it didn't shatter.

'Can I ask you something else?' George moved closer to the salesman. 'What is this 4DX?'

'Sir, it's a model of the JCB. It's a construction excavator. The JCBs we normally see are the 3DX model. The 4DX has a larger trunk—that is, the excavator is elongated.' The salesman waited for George's next question, but George had learned enough.

George took out two thousand rupees from his wallet, flashed it in the air, and handed over the money to the salesman. The salesman hesitated to accept it, but George pushed the money into his palms. George and Anand wasted no time in leaving the store. They forgot about the car battery.

Once outside, George first called Anthony. His phone was switched off. He then dialled Senapathy.

'George, good afternoon! I am busy right now. Can I call you back in thirty minutes?'

Senapathy was always courteous to George. George's report about the loopholes in the security around Area 11 had impressed him.

George scratched his head. 'Okay, sir … please call me when you are free. I have something very important to discuss.'

Anand noted George's restlessness and smiled. George always preached that patience was an investigator's greatest virtue.

'If it's that important, let's talk now.'

'Sir, I need a list of JCBs that were in operation inside Area 11 and outside the walls when Mandal went missing. A list of drivers, cleaners … And I need to know if any of the operators quit work after this incident. Any little detail would be useful. Sir, this is very important.'

Senapathy promised a speedy investigation and hung up.

The weather outside was as pleasant as George's current mental state. The sun wasn't too harsh that day. They roamed around the town and then began the commute home.

Anand stopped at a sugarcane juice shop. 'Sir, why didn't you specifically mention 4DX when you asked Senapathy sir about JCBs? Wouldn't things have gotten easier?'

'If we reveal everything and things don't go the way we expect them to, we would be disappointed. Even otherwise, think about it, Anand. You are in an accident caused by a JCB driver. If you call me to give the information, wouldn't you just say JCB? Would you say 4DX? How many people would understand that? I am excited about the clue. But I am also beginning to wonder if this could be a rather weak link.'

George raised his hand to signal to the waiter.

Anand pulled up a chair for George, and then said to the waiter, 'Son, a Titanic for me!'

'Titanic? What's that?' George cleaned the seat of the chair with his handkerchief.

'It's a special drink sold here. Regular sugarcane juice but with lots of ice.'

Anand made faces, hoping to make a baby across from them laugh. But the child started bawling instead and turned his back on them, holding tightly onto his mother.

'Why a name like Titanic?' George asked.

'Probably because of the ice overload? If I tell you something now, will you be shocked?'

George shook his head, feeling uncomfortable looking at the flies hovering around the sugarcane crusher.

'Sir, we know a JCB driver who quit his job at Area 11: Satyajit. Sahadevan told us he worked at the dumping yard, and that he helped people smuggle many things outside the property. There was a cleaner with him, a fellow who behaved badly with women. Sahadevan kept saying, "If Satyajit were here ..." Doesn't that mean Satyajit is no longer at Area 11?'

George took Anand's hand. 'You remember even the tiniest of details. Your memory is great, and I always value people who can summon the right detail at the right time. But right now, we've both forgotten one thing. About the car battery that we were supposed to collect!'

The two of them burst out laughing. Done with crying, the baby at the next table also joined in.

It was past nine when Anthony came in with details of the drivers.

Anand called out to him as he opened the gate. 'What happened? Were you mining the earth for all this information? It has been a long time since we called.'

'These are not details we could get off a computer. We had to plough through old registers and records. Nothing moves at the gate until the four hundred temporary employees sign out after their shift. Forget Senapathy, even if God called in on a direct line, he could not have got the information quickly. Everybody was too busy.'

Anthony parked his bike on the porch and came in with two large envelopes.

'Three people have stopped coming to work since the incident. The first name is important: Abdul. People call him Bhaijaan. He stopped working fourteen days after Mandal went missing. We hear he has gone back to his hometown.'

Anthony handed over the first envelope to George.

'Why do you think he is important?'

George didn't open the envelope, but placed it on the coffee table.

'Both Abdul and Mandal are from Uttar Pradesh. His village, Malwa, is only three kilometres away from Mandal's hometown.'

George, who was listening attentively, asked Anthony to sit down.

'The second person, Kodumudi, is from Tamil Nadu. He didn't have a license. He got in through some contacts at the firm where he worked earlier. His address is not in the records.'

Anthony placed the second envelope on the coffee table.

'This Kodumudi normally works only for a month. Once he earns enough money, he goes back home and then returns after months. Quitting a job without notice is what he regularly does. The third person of interest is from Ernakulam. Satyajit. He hasn't entered Area 11 since the day Mandal went missing. I have photographs of the three of them here. They were taken in order to issue them their entry passes. So, image clarity would be a problem.'

Anthony leaned back on the sofa, relaxing after a hard day's work. George took out Satyajit's photo and put it on the table. A middle-aged man with spots of grey in his hair and beard.

George began clicking pictures of Satyajit's photograph using his phone. 'Do you know this Satyajit well?'

'I have seen all three of them. Maybe more of Satyajit because he worked at the dumping yard. I haven't spoken to any of them, though.'

'Have you noticed anything peculiar about the excavator he drives? Take your time. Think about it.'

'Well, come to think of it … the arms of his JCB are longer. Which is why it is used in the dumping yard.'

George's face lit up, and his voice became eager. 'How is such a vehicle used in the dumping yard?'

'This dumping yard is not restricted to the area you saw. When you came to see it, sir, it must have seemed like an acre-wide area. The top of a hill was shaved off to create the yard. The original area should be about ten cents. The rest of the area was created by binding soil on top of dried leaves and green waste from Area 11. That is how the government operates when it takes over waste management. Now, there are stacks of dried leaves as high as a ten-storey building under the soil. The earth gets spongy as you get to the edges. So, a tipper deposits the leaves at the end, and a JCB pulls it into the yard. Hiring a JCB for this task costs around ten thousand rupees a day, and there is rent on top of that. Earlier, it was common for the JCBs to sink into the earth. We had to get cranes from outside to pull them out. It would take about two to three weeks to organise the paper and permissions for that. The JCB would be trapped inside for that long. So, no one would send their excavators to work in the dumping yard. That is why we hired this vehicle from Ernakulam. With this kind of excavator, the waste can be dropped into pits from a long distance away. Its arms are longer.'

'Anthony, can you tell me everything you know about Satyajit? Even things that you may feel are irrelevant. Every tiny detail.'

Anthony got up to check on Anand in the kitchen.

'Honestly, I don't know much about him. He tried to smile at me once or twice, but I ignored him. To find out more about him, you will have to catch hold of Sahadevan or someone else.'

That night, a restless George couldn't sleep until late. He woke up tired, later than usual. Anthony had some news for him by then. He was waiting in the living room, along with a cop who worked with Sub Inspector Amarnath.

'We checked the address Satyajit gave. There have been no signs of habitation in the house for at least eight years. The house looks like it is about to collapse any minute. Some of the neighbours don't even know anyone called Satyajit. He has no family. All he had was a father, who jumped in front of a train and committed suicide. This was about eight years ago when he was diagnosed with some disease. Amarnath sir dug up this information.'

The cop drank the coffee Anand gave him and made a quick exit. George was expressionless when he heard about Satyajit. He had expected exactly this. His guess about Abdul didn't miss the mark either. Abdul had got married and his wife's family didn't like the idea of him being a driver. They set up a mobile phone store for him. He was running it back in his hometown and leading a generally peaceful life. Anthony shared his current number and location. George didn't think he needed it. He was going to focus on Satyajit.

George gulped down breakfast and got ready to go out. Anthony sat in the driver's seat, without asking where they were headed. He would soon regret that. 'I would have taken my bike had I known we were coming here. What a fool I am. I should have asked. What a pain!' Anthony cursed himself.

They walked along narrow, slushy paths in search of Sahadevan's house. It turned out to be a wasted effort. Sahadevan had left home by then. He was assisting a cook at a wedding feast that day.

Anand folded his pants up to his knees. 'How is it so slushy here when we haven't had a drop of rain recently?'

Anthony ignored him, and a curious Anand repeated his question.

'Eda … this is not rainwater. There's a boy's hostel in Area 11 with a towering septic tank that leaks, and this place is always mucky as a result.' Anthony felt the sour taste of puke rise up his throat. He quietly swallowed.

On their way out, Anand kept thinking about what Anthony had told him. He felt nauseous. He felt a tinge of resentment, and some sympathy, towards Sahadevan. George was determined to meet Sahadevan that very day. That's just the way George was. He went after what he aimed to achieve, like a hound that wouldn't rest until it found its prey.

They caught up with Sahadevan as he was getting ready to chop onions, his knife held up like a magician's wand.

'Sir, I have no idea where Satyajit is. I met him when he was living here. He was just an acquaintance,' Sahadevan said.

'A girl from this town has gone missing. Aren't you also anxious to uncover the truth behind the incident?' George moved closer to him, almost whispering.

'I will be happy to tell you what I know. But honestly, I don't know where he is,' Sahadevan replied, seeming on the verge of tears.

'Okay. Listen carefully to what I am about to ask. You can think about it and then answer. At any time, did Satyajit work alone in the dumping yard?'

'No, sir. We work there from seven in the morning to six in the evening. Satyajit's shift was from 10 a.m. to 5 p.m. He was never alone in the dumping yard.'

'Was there any circumstance under which he had to work alone in the yard? Think carefully,' George pressed, taking Sahadevan's knife to give the onions a go. Sahadevan stuck to his answer.

Anand slipped in a question. 'You said he had a helper, the one who assaulted women. Where is he? Is there any way we can find him?'

'I don't know where exactly he lives. But I know his house is somewhere in this region itself. He used to come on a scooter daily. The registration number is from this area,' Sahadevan replied.

Anthony came up with an idea. 'Sir, we could search for Akhil on social media. I can recognise him by his picture. We can find out his address or some other detail.'

Sahadevan perked up. 'It must be him, sir. Satyajit is a poor thing. But this Akhil … he has the look of a murderer. His face looks beastly. He is a thief. Like Anthony sir said, you can check on the internet. He has written a book and all that.'

George stopped chopping onions. 'Book? What book?'

'Oh, that? I don't know the name and all that. I have heard people mention it. The title has something to do with marijuana.'

'Weed? These people are trouble. Right, Anand?' George remarked, getting up to leave.

'Sir …' Sahadevan called out. George turned around. He was expecting that call.

'Sir, there was this one day when Satyajit was alone in the dumping yard. It was his daughter's birthday. So, he bought us lunch. In the middle of the meal, he got a phone call, saying there was an urgent job. He told us he was going to the dumping yard.'

Sahadevan wondered why he hadn't thought of this earlier. 'Normally, no one is called into the yard during that time. 1–3 p.m. is break time when no manual work happens around Area 11. I remember we had discussed this at the hotel. But somehow, I forgot about this when you asked me earlier.'

'Had Satyajit invited you to the birthday celebration well in advance? The previous day, or even earlier, perhaps?'

'No, sir. He told us about it at around 11 a.m. that day, when we were on our tea break. We had all got lunch from home, but we didn't want to throw away the chance to eat the occasional good meal. So, we dumped our packed lunches in the waste. For the past week, there were a lot of biryani leftovers coming into the yard. So, I was tempted to eat meat. Everything worked in our favour that day. Do you know the ground where they park taxis, next to the Jammu circle? We went to a big hotel there. Satyan got a call as we began to eat. He left. We had to wait until he returned. We had come to the hotel in a tipper, and he had used it to return to the dumping yard.'

George looked into Sahadevan's eyes. 'When you came back from the hotel, did you notice anything different in the dumping yard?'

'I never got the time to notice anything, sir. We returned very late. The women workers were cursing us for our gluttony. We were very late, the shift was over. I didn't even have to change into my work clothes.'

'Okay … Sahadevan, do you drink?'

'A bit. Only when I am on leave, sir.'

'Then, can you come to the car with me? I will give you some stuff. Drink a bit. You will be on leave tomorrow.' George winked at Anand and walked to the car.

That night, George opened a bottle identical to the one he had given Sahadevan. Anand was pouring some liquor into a glass when the doorbell rang. Anthony was outside, along with a stranger.

'I have hung around you so much that I too have become Sherlock. I caught hold of someone. Just check.'

The stranger grew nervous at the sight of alcohol. Even Anthony hadn't expected the bottle.

'Sir, this is Baasith. You know the hotel in front of our gate? He cooks parottas there and sometimes doubles up as a waiter. I asked him about Satyajit. Even he hasn't seen him since that day. But he said something else. About two weeks before Ashwini disappeared, she had given Satyajit a tight slap. He witnessed that. Tell him, Baasith. Sir is our man. You have nothing to fear.'

George asked Baasith to sit down.

'Satyan used to wash his vehicle in front of the hotel. Once, when he threw away the dirty, soapy water after a wash, it fell on this woman's clothes. They exchanged a few words. I couldn't hear what they said. But soon, she gave him a resounding slap. I heard it from a distance. Satyajit stood frozen.'

'You say this happened in front of the hotel … did no one else see this? No one else has spoken about this so far,' George said, as he signalled to Anand to remove the bottle and the glasses.

Baasith was on the edge of his seat. 'It was very crowded. But no one else seemed to have noticed this incident.'

Anand was miffed that he had missed his chance to have a drink. 'How can that be, son? If it happened in front of your hotel, wouldn't someone else also have seen it?'

'They were on the road. The road is overgrown with bushes. I had gone there for a smoke. There was a national permit lorry parked close to them. That lorry hid them from view. Had anyone seen them, they would have killed her and chopped her into sixteen pieces. None of the workers liked her.'

'Why didn't the workers like her?' George asked.

'She is filthy rich. Very haughty and stuck-up because of that. She wears clothes no one here wears. Then—' Baasith hesitated.

Anthony encouraged him. 'Continue … don't hesitate. You have nothing to fear.'

'Sometimes, a guy drops her on his Duke. She gets off the bike and gives him a kiss and all. She doesn't care that the world is watching. The workers don't like this kind of behaviour.'

Baasith seemed eager to disappear from the scene. Anthony gave Baasith the key to his bike. 'You may leave.' George gave him two thousand rupees, but Baasith didn't accept it.

'No, sir. My work pays me enough.' George watched Baasith walk out, the bike keys dangling from his ring finger.

George turned out to be right. The next day was a holiday for Sahadevan. All the dumping yard employees were told to stay home, and police barricaded the area. Some senior officers and cadets under fifteen were the only ones in the yard. Senapathy and Shyamaprasad sat under a tree, inspecting the activities from a distance. Anthony jogged his memory and marked the spots where waste had been dumped on the days after the duo went missing. George wanted those spots to be dug up first.

The JCB excavator that Satyajit drove was brought in. A handsome young man who wore the same uniform as Senapathy was at the wheel. George was happy to see the speed and expertise with which he operated the excavator. An hour into the search, a whistle sounded from a ditch dug up by the JCB. The man assigned to inspect the work near the ditch blew the whistle two more times. Senapathy and George rushed forward. But they were asked to keep away from the ditch. The risk of the earth collapsing around it was too great. Two men descended into the ditch with ropes, sickles and hooks. In about five minutes, their job was done. Everyone outside held their breath. One more long whistle resounded through the air. With a rumble, the JCB spat out a large plastic bag caught in its teeth.

Inside the bag, they found what they expected to find. Even then, the sight was too gruesome. A long, blue plastic bag. Two skeletons. The bodies had almost entirely decomposed and only parts of their clothes were intact. Everyone first noticed the scraps of Mandal's uniform. People backed away. After a doctor's initial examination, the bodies, or what was left of them, were moved to an ambulance.

George and Shyamaprasad led a distraught Senapathy to his car. Senapathy knew they had come this far because of George's relentless pursuit. He wished to thank George. But the sight of his former colleague's body had numbed him. The words he wanted to articulate felt as if they were stuck in his throat. He looked at George with eyes full of sorrow. Shyamaprasad gently shut the door of the car. Senapathy sunk back into his seat.

Soon, he addressed the new investigation team. He ended his long speech with a call. 'We need to find Mandal's killer at any cost. That's a given. This is not only about the lost honour of Area 11. Whoever came in here, and messed with our boy so easily … I want him caught.'

Senapathy was a man who could attract people to a cause. His voice was fraught with emotion, and everyone in the room made it their mission to find Satyajit.

Senapathy formed an eleven-member squad comprising Area 11 security officers and Kerala Police. George, Anthony and Anand formed a parallel team reporting to Senapathy. Anthony knew more about the security systems in Area 11 than anyone else. He was also the only one among them who had seen Satyajit in person.

After the meeting, George wanted to go with Anthony to his house to pick up some clothes. But there was a line of officers of various ranks eager to meet George. He had to spend a lot of time meeting them. They all interacted with George gingerly for he was famous for his volatile temper. For George, the conversations came as a break from the stress of the past few weeks.

On the way home, Anthony was in the driver's seat. His presence made it easier for them to escape the checkpoints. Anthony was also the most familiar with the shortcuts and pathways. George thought that the routes within Area 11 were like a man's mind—there were more hidden alleys than main roads.

Police vehicles were stationed along their route. The speed limit within the area was forty kilometres per hour. The slow pace let Anand savour the sights. He liked the order and cleanliness around him. There were large shady trees on either side of the street, but not one dry leaf beneath. The endless expanse of tamed green gave way to the ocean. Anand was immersed in the atmosphere.

George, too, was deep in thought. A question from Anthony broke the silence. 'Sir, how were you so sure that we would find the bodies in the dumping yard?'

'Right at the outset, I believed that they fell into danger by the wilderness near the dumping yard. CCTV records showed they were last seen near the area. From the time our investigation led us to a JCB, I was sure that it was used to bury the bodies. If the murderer could operate a JCB, it was an educated guess that he would use it. The pathway in the wilderness is so dense that not even a bike can go through it. The last place where a large vehicle can be used is the dumping yard. The dumping yard had its advantage. The signs of a freshly dug ditch would not raise any alarm. It is normal to dig a ditch and then cover it up in the yard. There is an added advantage. The stench from a rotting corpse will go unnoticed in a place where there is a constant unpleasant smell.

'When Sahadevan told us about how Satyajit went alone to the yard in the middle of the lunch he was hosting, I was convinced. If he were planning to give a treat, he would have informed the workers earlier; he knew that everyone brought packed lunch from home. From this, I surmised that the murder did take place in the yard, but that the murderer didn't have enough time to plan the crime. A previous enmity or some other motive we don't yet know about led to this crime.

'The girl who was murdered was on leave for four days before her death. She was at her cousin's wedding. I asked around if any changes had taken place in Area 11 during those four days, but I got nowhere with that line of questioning. I narrowed my search to that small pathway in the wilderness.

I found something interesting. Three days before the woman returned from leave, one part of that path was closed with crude boulders. An officer in charge of the dumping yard had closed the path fearing it would create security problems. Regular commuters stopped using the pathway in a day or two but the alley near the helicopter display was still open. The officer thought it would be sufficient to close the route from one side alone so that it was rendered unusable. Had both ends been sealed, two lives would have been saved.

'Mandal was not a regular commuter on this route so he was unaware of the closure. Ashwini had been on leave for a few days before the closure, and so she, too, wasn't aware. We can guess what happened next. Satyajit would have seen Ashwini walking down the path alone. He knew that no one else would walk that way. His motive, perhaps, was rage. We know that she had slapped him in front of the hotel. We don't know why she had reacted so violently. There may have been a history between them. We are all heirs to the legacy of slavery. Our rage erupts when someone has tested our patience beyond a point. Perhaps, finding her alone, he tried to assault her. It's possible that Mandal walked by that way just then. Or, Mandal may have seen Satyajit when he was trying to cover up the body. He would surely have interrupted Satyajit. The only fact we know is that she had to share her burial ground with him.'

Anthony slowed the car down in front of a large bungalow with a high gate. 'Don't we have to check on that cleaner chap?' Anand reminded George about Akhil.

'He may have played a part in helping Satyajit hide. But he doesn't have a hand in the murders. He was driving an ambulance to Kochi naval base at that time to deliver medicines. Maybe that was a good thing. The young woman may have suffered a lot more if there had been two of them.'

George and Anand got out of the car after Anthony. 'Mamma is at the gym. The house is generally empty this time of the day.'

Anthony walked to the tall, intricately carved wooden door with his key.

'Where's your father?' asked Anand. Anthony ignored the question.

The answer to that question came in the form of a large ten-foot photograph that greeted them when they entered the house. Against a backdrop of warplanes stood a tall officer with multiple medals decorating his uniform. An astonished Anand stared at Senapathy's smiling face. He gazed at the picture for a long time, looking for a resemblance to Anthony.

A twenty-four-day-long investigation could not lead them anywhere near Satyajit. Despite their intense efforts, George and the team had no clue where the man was hiding.

'Let's take the day off today. We need to go to Thuravoor police station. Old vehicles are being moved for auction there. There is an old Ambassador there, I want to buy it. That car was the hero in the first case I ever cracked. The driver was murdered by people who had rented the car. Also, I need to thank SI Amarnath. He was the one who first gathered details on Satyajit after a call to Ernakulam.' George got a bottle of water from the refrigerator and banged the door shut.

'A police station on our day off? What a charmed life we lead!' Anand gritted his teeth as he emptied a packet of mango pickle into a jar.

At the police station, two young women were distributing cake. Amarnath's car was outside, but he was away with another SI at the Thalassery Court. It was a long wait. The women passed by George and Anand, but didn't offer them any cake. They were not in uniform, after all. Anand presumed that one of them was celebrating their birthday.

Anand was restless. 'Let me see if I can get a piece of cake for us!' He went inside the station.

About two minutes later, George saw Anthony rush into the station like a man with a purpose. Amarnath's Jeep entered the station at the same time. So, he couldn't immediately follow Anthony inside.

As soon as Amarnath got out of the car, he brushed aside a couple of people trying to talk to him and approached George. He had a big smile on his face and was about to speak when Anand rushed out of the station and interrupted them.

'Oof, where did you find that person? The one in the soiled mundu? The man on the bench.'

Amarnath looked at him, puzzled. 'Oh … that's not a big case. A few sundry thefts and illegal hooch. But the villagers have smashed him into a pulp.'

'Ha! Adipoli!' exclaimed Anand. 'We cast a net and waited patiently, but we couldn't catch him. Now, the idiot lands right in front of us when we least expected it. He's that fellow, sir. Satyajit. Anthony saw him and confirmed his identity.'

George made to dash into the next room. Then he abruptly stopped and turned around.

'SI Amarnath, I need a favour. Could you talk to him? Make it seem like he was caught at my behest?'

Amarnath adjusted his cap and followed him. 'That's not a problem, sir. But if this case brings you name and fame, don't forget us!'

Inside the hall on the left side, a young man sat crouched on a bench, a helmet in his hands. The old bench was hollowed out in the middle. Amarnath glowered at him.

'Eda, why are you turning away your face? Am I your girlfriend or what?'

Satyajit's clothes were smeared with dirt and blood. He tried to get up. SI Amarnath lent him a hand, and then turned to George.

'I had him in my sights for a week, but I didn't catch him because you asked me not to, sir. If I had delayed it any further, the villagers would have been on my case. That's why we grabbed him and put him in the Jeep. Just because you asked us to, we haven't touched him so far. All this blood is the contribution of the village mob.'

Satyajit's eyes turned to George. As if on cue, SI Amarnath left the room. George sat down on the bench next to Satyajit.

Satyajit's voice was low. He grimaced as he spoke through a split lip. 'Sir, I didn't steal anything.'

'I know. Even if you stole something, it's no big deal. Petty thefts, making liquor out of a few cashew fruits … are they big crimes? Forget all that. I need a favour from you, Satyan. I have a job that involves a JCB. Forget your regular hourly rate, I will pay you what you ask for. First, we need to dig a ditch. It's a secret matter. That's why I especially sought you out.'

Satyajit struggled to speak. 'What kind of ditch, sir?'

'A small ditch. A girl who lives next door was finished because of a small mistake I made. I didn't intend to kill her. It was an accident. But that's not the real problem. A fellow who was passing by witnessed the act. I had no option but to finish him off as well. If the bodies are destroyed, there won't be a case. We'll dig a ditch and dump them both in there. Not a big hole. Do you remember the ditch you dug at the dumping yard? That depth would be perfect. What do you say? Are you in?'

Satyan swallowed, and began to shiver.

George waited a few minutes. There was no answer. He couldn't even hear Satyajit breathing.

'I know every little detail.' George's voice turned menacing. 'I won't tell anyone the truth, but I will perform a little surgery on the truth I know. I will say that you killed the officer because you wanted his weapon. On Republic Day, a new batch of cadets will complete their training. A mass slaughter with that machine gun—that was your plan. That is why you sneaked your way into Area 11. You have hidden the gun within Area 11 so that you can retrieve it when you want. That woman, Ashwini, saw you murder Mandal. It was only natural that you took her out to protect yourself. Would the one who steals an ox hesitate to steal an egg? I will say that no matter how cruelly I torture you, you will not reveal where you hid the gun. Because even if you cannot carry out this mass murder yourself, you have a proxy in Area 11. I could spin the story this way. Even if you sweat it out, you cannot prove that I am wrong.'

'Sir, they will kill me.'

'I will help you. I am not saying that I will save you from the police. That would be a lie, and I don't like to lie. Area 11 cops will pick you up from here immediately. If Anthony's phone is working fine, they should be on their way already. If you don't cooperate with me, I will tell them the truth. But if you do as I say, I will dilute the truth and I will stand by you. I want the machine gun you have stolen. If you give me that, I will stand by you.'

'Sir, that gun is not with me.' Satyajit's reply was swift. George looked around the police station with a sigh. He got up from the bench. His trousers were too loose for him. He pulled them back up to his waist.

'Okay, Satyajit, in that case, I have to turn against you. Try fighting me, and I'll show you what I can do.'

Satyajit fell at George's feet. 'I am telling you the truth, sir. It's been two days since the gun went missing from my hiding place. If I had the gun with me, I wouldn't have been caught. I was careless. I swear on my steering wheel, sir, the damn weapon is not with me. Don't let me get caught. They will kill me, sir.'

George turned to look at Satyajit, who said, 'It's true, sir. Along with the gun, I also lost twenty-four lakh rupees.' He wouldn't let go of George's leg.

Later, SI Amarnath accompanied George to the car. 'There's a hilly area near Area 11. Ekarmala. They called the region Ettunaad. It is not a place that comes under the jurisdiction of this station. But this is the only place through which they have an approach road. They have their own police force. They call it the Ettunaad Army. They have no respect for us. Both men and women there are all crazy and violent. If you are going there, you have to be very careful. That place has a violent history.'

Anthony repeated an old story. 'When we first came here, Mamma wanted to see a Theyyam performance. We had gone to Ettunaad then. They call it Theyyam, but what they really do is roast men alive. My mother almost fainted. We were seated a bit far away. But a stray ember flew and landed on my father's arm. He still has a black scar there. What SI Amarnath said is correct. Everybody there is crazy. Searching for a man there will be like looking for a needle in a haystack. And you are only looking for a gun! Don't go there. My advice would be to send the cops from Area 11.'

'No! We need to go there,' George was firm.

'When Amar narrated the history of Ettunaad, I thought about the connection our case has to that town. The village from which Mandal's father hailed. My gut says there are a lot of missing pieces in this puzzle. The truth could be beyond what we found out and what Amar just told us.'

On the way back from the police station, Anthony stopped by a beautiful valley. He looked relaxed now.

Anand got down from the car and began to seek a spot to urinate in. He then quipped, 'George sir, if you go there, you'll find the gun easily. You rely on luck and coincidence as much as brains. 4DX that day. And Satyan today. Who knows—the gun, too, might fall into your hands!'

George, having climbed down a rock to take in the view, responded thoughtfully, 'Hard work is always aided by good fortune. That's what happened here.'

He continued walking further down to enjoy the breathtaking vista of hills and the endless expanse of mountains beyond.

Moving Pyre

Achchan Namboodiri called out to all the gods he knew for an escape route.

Two men stood in front of him with an ordinary iron trunk held up by hand-spun towels on both sides. The men holding the trunk wore the cheap tiger masks sold at temple festival fairs. One fellow was reed thin, while the other was rotund. The stout man certainly hadn't been seen in the village before. They looked comical in their masks, but Achchan Namboodiri was in no mood to laugh.

The iron trunk was rusting at the sides and beginning to crumble in the middle. There was nothing spectacular about it. But one look at the box and Achchan Namboodiri got so scared that he even forgot the names of his favourite gods. He wept and bowed before the intruders with folded hands. It was a pathetic sight. It didn't, however, move the Lion in front of him who stood still as a statue. The third intruder, a man with a blood-splattered lion mask, did not look comical. His dreadlocks were stiff with dried blood.

Achchan Namboodiri fell at his feet and begged the creature to spare his life. One of the tigers pulled out a long knife tucked into his back. It wasn't as flexible as a machete but it was enough to knock down the weak Achchan Namboodiri.

The tiger took a few steps forward. Achchan Namboodiri felt his legs turn into jelly. He imagined the weapon tearing into his flesh. He shut his eyes. Then he heard the knife slice into a fat banana tree that had withstood heavy winds and stood strong on the riverbank.

The tiger tore into the trunk of the banana tree, with his fingers deftly extracting the pith along with the sheath of leaves. Achchan Namboodiri understood what was happening. He fell on the sand, thrashing his limbs as if he had been stabbed. The lion untied a gold-bordered mundu from his head, and hurled the garment on the sand. In a few seconds, the two men with the tiger masks tied up Achchan Namboodiri's hands with the shimmering cloth.

'Don't kill me! I have made a mistake. I am sorry. I am an old man now — a fragile person. I am already being punished for what I did. I am just an old man. Don't punish me again. I will fall at your feet. Don't kill me.'

Despite the tight knots, Achchan Namboodiri folded his palms to seek forgiveness.

Behind him, the tiger's voice was full of sarcasm. 'All your strength and valour are finished. You have come to me as a weak man. There is a saying in Sanskrit. You may not have heard of it. Horses and elephants are never offered as sacrifices. A tiger is never chosen. Only the goat is sacrificed in any ritual. Even God destroys the weak.'

Achchan Namboodiri's folded palms fell to the ground. The tiger placed the banana stem on Namboodiri's naked chest and tied it tightly with the banana fibre.

The tiger gave him a mock blessing. 'The banana stem purifies the blood and gets rid of Raktha Dosha. Let this stem remove your dosha.'

Namboodiri crawled on the floor, begging and pleading, and reached the Lion. He rubbed his face against the Lion's feet. 'Please save me!'

'Why should I save you? What relationship do you and I have?' The Lion's voice echoed against the stones on the riverbank. 'You determined the time of your death in a previous story. I am only a middleman.'

The Lion locked his hands behind his back. Cries of 'Hear, Hear' erupted from the tigers. The Lion then spread out his fingers, gesturing to them to open the box.

Achchan Namboodiri's fears came true. The embers under the firewood stove in the box glowed like a diamond when exposed to the wind. The lion grabbed a handful of embers with his bare hands and stepped forward. With long silver nails adorning his fingers, he placed the smouldering cinders on the banana stems lying on Namboodiri's chest.

The lion cupped his right palm over his ear as if he were listening intently. Achchan Namboodiri's shrieks of pain were louder than he had expected. The tigers scooped up the cinders with ladles covered in cloth. They seemed to compete to see who would pour more embers onto Achchan Namboodiri's chest. The victim of their ire lay writhing in the sand, his body contorted. His piercing cries were music to the lion's ears. Drunk on joy, he playfully tried a few awkward dance steps on the wet sand.

Achchan Namboodiri's body drifted along the strong currents of the Vannathi river for a long time. It was 3.30 a.m. when the sand miners spotted him. Glowing embers seemed to adorn the body. Utthaman, a sand miner, thought a large star was floating towards him. His companion Vijayan thought that a Theyyam was walking on water with many flambeaus on his headdress. There was a Theyyam shrine in that part of the riverbank.

They stopped work as the boat inched closer. Both their guesses turned out to be wrong. They stared in astonishment as they saw a corpse with flaming torches all over its body floating towards them. Vijayan summoned courage and flashed his searchlight on the corpse's face. He recognised the man and almost lost his footing in shock. Uttaman held on tight to steady him.

They took out their phones, which were wrapped in plastic to protect them from the water, and made a call to the shore. The body had floated over a bend in the river and was beyond their line of vision by then.

The people who saw that unusual moving pyre were many. Sand miners and a few fishermen. Drivers waiting on the riverbank. People returning home after a night of forbidden activities. Workers transporting milk. Enthusiastic morning walkers. The night birds.

Word spread through phone calls, and a large group of people gathered as if for a boat race. There was no space for more on both banks of the river. When the corpse came closer, no one dared to go ahead and stop the body from floating or bring the body ashore.

Finally, the branches of a tree on the river bend did the job and stopped the corpse from floating away. As day broke, the riverbank was packed with curious onlookers.

Raghavan felt that he had never seen such a large crowd, even during the season when the local Theyyam, Irumukhan, made an appearance. By the time Achchan Namboodiri was brought to the shore, the flames had run out. He looked like a porcupine with charred sticks all over his body.

When George went closer to the body, he saw that the corpse was almost entirely burnt. The stumps that protruded from the body looked like disobedient body hair. The stumps, George noticed, were all twigs from the vaar tree.

It was the powerful Namboodiri who had died. After a long time, Ettunaad experienced the autocracy of the police force. Many people stayed home out of fear. A police Jeep picked up people walking on the streets or loitering around the market. The cops got carried away and even barged into some homes.

Pachila Korachchan was among those who got caught in the police net at Nagathaanam Bend. Someone stopped cops on their way and told the SI that Korachchan was among the town's venerated elders. The SI apologised, bought Korachchan a biryani and sent him home in another police Jeep. Luckily for the SI, the villagers of Perunthatta got to know about Korachchan's detention only after he was home.

At the tea-shop, Mooshaari was up to his tricks. 'Chindachchan is not dead. He still lives among us. I have felt his presence many times. Many of you still remember how a *firangi* lady pushed me down and attacked me on the sand. I know, I know. Some of you still tease me about it. But now I say: That was no *firangi*. No *Madaama*. Chindachchan's ghost had come to me in the form of a white woman. To kick me and drag me to the river, the *Madaama* had done some Kalari moves. My eyes nearly popped out. Only Chindachchan knew those moves. When I saw how flexible she was, I knew she was Chindachchan himself. My mind was full of devotion at that moment. Which is why I deliberately fell into the river. I ingested a lot of water. You won't believe this, but that day … the water was extremely sweet. That young woman was Chindachchan. Otherwise, do you think a woman can physically assault a man like Mooshaari?'

Mooshaari looked around slyly to see the crowd's reaction to his monologue.

Rahul's reply hit him where it hurt. 'Are you saying a woman can't physically assault you? Is that why Sumathi Chechi kicked you into a marsh?'

Laughter rang out from all four corners of the tea shop.

'That was Sumathi. Leave her out. She is not a woman.' Mooshaari tried to look stoic. But everyone in the shop laughed at his embarrassment.

He continued to grumble: 'Sumathi is not a woman. I am sure of that.'

Bhashim Bhaiyya, who had migrated to Ettunaad from Assam many years ago to work in a quarry, wanted to contradict that claim about Sumathi. But having experienced several blows from the hoodlums of Ettunaad, he reined his words in.

'Why are these toddlers sitting in the tea shop? Raghava, isn't this fellow your nephew? You have a thousand tongues when it comes to the affairs of other people.' Everyone knew Mooshaari was trying to silence Rahul for talking about

Sumathi. Those who didn't like Mooshaari were tempted to provoke him further.

'Calm down, Mooshaari. This is a tea shop, not a bar. Even young people are welcome here.' Balakrishnan's timely interjection ruined an opportunity for a good fight.

Balan, who was soaking the dirty glasses in soap water, said, 'The people of Ettunaad never needed reasons to pick a fight with each other. Now, they don't need reasons to die either.'

'Who said people are dying without reason? Whoever betrayed Chindachchan is in line to get assaulted. Even Kangaani, who drove him to the hospital that day, was found dead in a well with his head split open. Take the case of Dasan, who hitched a ride on the Jeep that day. His wife went mad and died. His house was mortgaged. He fled town, and now, no one knows whether he's dead or alive. That Nandanar is still cooped up in his house. They say he has gone mad. The poor thing's job was to tear tickets at the theatre as moviegoers came in. Now, Chindachchan has torn his ticket. Among those who drove Chindachchan to the hospital, only Giri and Raghavettan are alive ...' Sajith, the tempo driver, got started on a topic that everyone in the shop was keen to discuss. Those who were lingering outside the shop quickly walked in to listen.

'But still ... why trouble Nandanar so much for a word he used accidentally?' Many in the shop had pondered the same question as Balakrishnan.

'Spirits attack everyone they were connected to. Ghosts don't have the power to distinguish between good and bad memories.' Naanu Carpenter, who was in the habit of nursing a glass of black coffee for hours, spoke up after a long time. He was a man of few words. He was conscious of his effeminate voice and hated to be mocked for it.

Balan made his way back to the conversation, holding hot tea in glasses that were barely washed. 'Ghosts don't have a good memory, it seems. How do you say that so confidently? Did a ghost sit with you on the same bench in Class II? What theories! I strongly suspect that useless fellow. I doubt if he would be brave enough to kill Achchan Namboodiri. But I am sure of one thing. That fellow is a King Cobra.'

'Whether it's a ghost or a man, we know one thing. The creature is punctilious and meticulous. Raghavetta, be prepared!' Sajith gulped down the rest of his tea, put a dusty towel over his shoulder, and got up to leave.

Someone from the crowd agreed. 'That is true. Giri is not in town. When he hears about what is happening, he is unlikely to be keen to return from the Gulf. But Raghavan is close enough to be attacked at any point in time.'

'It's not very hard to summon Giri here. Just stick a flaming torch up Giri's father, Keluvasan's chest, like how it was done for Achchan Namboodiri. Giri will arrive immediately.'

Kuttan, who was observing a fly swimming in his teacup, looked up when he heard this. He took a long hard look at the speaker, Sajith. Sajith had been saying his goodbyes and then lingering on at the tea shop for a long time now. When he finally left, Kuttan paid for the many cups of tea Sajith had downed that day.

Outside, Rahul struggled to catch up with his uncle Raghavan. 'Is there any truth in what people are saying, Ammaava? Do you know anything about how Chindachchan died?'

Raghavan was almost running, as if someone had lit a fire under him. 'Eda, what wrong are they saying I did? The custom is that attendants hold the ropes attached to the Theyyam when he is pulled away from the fire. The Theyyam can die of burns otherwise. Giri always held that rope. That was the level of trust Chindachchan placed in Giri. What happened next was between them. I adjusted my rhythm to Giri's. You know, right … when a rich man asks you to do something, you can't argue with that. I am telling this only to you. Keep it to yourself.'

Raghavan rubbed off a tea stain from his shirt and walked slower to keep pace with Rahul.

'Leave the rest of the story aside, Ammaava. In those days, Giri didn't even have five paisa to his name. How can you say that you were just following what a rich man did?'

Raghavan turned around and gave Rahul a withering look. Rahul went quiet and kept his head down. He looked up when he was sure Raghavan had gone some distance. By then, Raghavan had disappeared into an alley that was thick with foliage on both sides.

Anand and George were walking back to their room after stopping for tea at Balan's shop. 'Such gruesome murders … And how can they believe that the soul of a man long gone is committing these crimes, sir? It's too surprising.'

'Nothing to be surprised there. When there are rumours of mysterious sightings like the Blackman, people start claiming they have seen the creature. They say they saw the entity in an abandoned building, on a tree, etc., and people crowd the place out of curiosity. Eventually, what emerges is a dog or a black monkey. People believe anything in these parts. A society infected with fear loses the ability to think logically. But what they call 'Chindachchan' is not a smokescreen. There is a serial killer in these parts who believes that he is being guided by some supernatural force. He is playing the long game. He hasn't yet started killing for pleasure. Which is why you and I are still alive.'

'The man they mentioned, Dasan … he could be Mandal's father, right?' Anand asked. George barely acknowledged the question.

They climbed up some old, faded steps to reach the room. There was an old iron trunk waiting right outside the door. George looked at Anand and sat in front of the box. There was a note stuck to the rusty box. George felt the lid of the box and opened the letter.

'Do not look for me in Ettunaad. Those who seek me cannot see me. I am a submarine. While you search for me on the surface of the water, I will be deep inside, plotting to attack you. The eyes that are looking for me don't see me. But don't think I don't exist. I repeat, I am a submarine. One who is constantly at war. Don't approach me for a regular gun. Not one person who has faced my missiles is now alive. If you intend to stay here plying your fake timber trade and espionage, I will come after you. I am not a charitable person. But I donate to you the gun you are looking for, and three hours to leave this place. Ensure that this is our final encounter. Let me remind you: Expert hunters don't give anyone a second warning.'

Anand waited for George's permission to open the box. 'What could be inside this?'

'Either a wreath of flowers or the gun we are looking for!'

George passed on the letter to Anand and opened the box. He was right. The dismantled gun, its parts wrapped in cloth, lay in the box.

Anand read the letter and flung it aside as if it were an ember. 'Let's leave this place, sir. Haven't we found what we are looking for? Why should we wrestle with that cursed presence? I don't think any more murders will happen here. The cops are on alert. Every corner of the region is under their watch. In these unfavourable circumstances, I don't think this place will see one more murder. Why should we hang on here?'

'However strong the police presence, two more deaths will certainly happen here. First, Kudakkaran Raghavan's and then Girdhar's. If a man has set out for a kill, unfavourable circumstances won't make a difference to him. For a criminal, being in jail is the only unfavourable circumstance. Even then, don't people jump jail? "Unfavourable circumstances" is an excuse found only in the lazy man's dictionary.'

'I made enquiries in Mandal's hometown in UP. The story there is that his father died a year and a half ago. The witness testimony says he was hit by a Jeep during his morning walk. The driver of the Jeep fled the scene. There are no more details. Is there a connection between his death and the murders happening here? Perhaps, if we dig deeper, we might find something. But there are two problems. The first is that we don't really have much information. All we have is a head with no neck and some half-formed theories. The second issue is this: you don't need a complete picture of events to close an investigation. If that were the case, no case in the world would ever be solved.'

George asked Anand to close the box and looked for Shyamaprasad's number on his phone.

'Sir! Some good news! The gun is now in our custody. Oh, that's a long story, I will tell you when we meet. See you soon!'

'Baletta, I have brought a new tenant for the room George Police vacated.'

Aadi had come running into the tea shop as if it were a home. Balakrishnan was stumped. George had given him the keys only two minutes ago. How did this fellow get the news so fast?

A young man followed Aadi into the tea shop. His clothes were muddy, and he sat quietly in a corner. He was around twenty-five years old. He looked like an animal wallowing in the dirt.

'*Him*? Is he the tenant? Wasn't he among the hoochers whom the police took away? I can't let him stay here. Are you on an adopting spree like your father Chindan? Put this fellow in that crumbling orphanage of his. Or … haven't you rented a house? Take him there.'

'Don't say that, Baletta … Saravanan won't let me take him there. This young man has just got a job as a JCB driver at Saamy's quarry. He will pay you the rent on time.'

Aadi's pleading voice came as a surprise to Balakrishnan. His behaviour was unpredictable. The villagers always said he had a few screws loose.

Balan laid out a towel on the desk and climbed up. 'This man looks like a thief. Take him away from here. I need to close the shop.'

Aadi gnashed his teeth and called out: 'Saamy Anna …'

Saamy Annan came in. With a phone wedged between his shoulder and head, he was talking to someone while using a calculator with both hands.

'Ayyo! Saamiettan?' Balan jumped off the desk and ingratiatingly wiped a chair so that Saamy could sit down.

Saamy didn't take his ears off the phone. 'Baletta … four piping hot teas, please!'

Balan ran to the kitchen.

Saamy called out to the young stranger. 'Akhil, go call the driver, too. He loves his tea.'

The stranger nodded vigorously and stepped out.

Balan came in with steaming hot tea and Saamy finally cut the call. 'We are sending granite to Kozhikode. So the agents won't give me or my phone a rest until midnight.'

'You have a good reputation in this village, Saamietta. Why are you getting involved in these people's affairs?'

'What reputation, Baletta? When I came to this town in a mud-splattered lungi, everyone, you included, drove me away like I was a rabid dog. Only Chindachchan gave me a leg up back then. He can no longer be a Theyyam, but he is still my Deivam—my god. If his son needs a favour, I need to stop what I am doing and help him. Isn't that the right thing to do?'

Balan kept mum, but he muttered to himself in his head: 'In any case, that man only liked Tamils.' Balan put on a show of obsequiousness, but he inwardly cursed Aadi until Saamy finished his tea.

Aadi collected the keys to the room and made to leave the shop.

A curious Balan spoke up: 'We have been hearing that your Chindan is killing off his enemies, one by one. Will this stop only after Giri Muthalaly is dead and buried?'

'Didn't you just call him by his name, "Chindan"? Until you and all the rascals around here take Chindachchan's name with respect, nothing is going to end.'

Aadi glared at Balan and walked out into the darkness.

The Lion's Tale – 1

The rain brightened up dark, barely tarred roads and kissed the yards red with a profusion of fallen pagoda flowers. The gentle drumming of water on brick-paved courtyards was music to the ears. Ettunaad had well and truly changed into vibrant monsoon colours.

Relentless showers had pounded the red earth for hours when a goods lorry sank into the slush about a kilometre from Purapuri. The road was too narrow, and the two vehicles behind them had to stop too.

'Let's get down, sir. Unlikely that this vehicle will move before sunrise.' Kaanaadi stepped on the muddy tyre and slid down. He gave a hand to the passenger to help him get off the road.

'Sir, what did you say your name was?' He asked the stranger for the fourteenth time.

'Morgan Freeman'

The man who called himself Morgan strapped his shoes to the sling of his rucksack. He watched the contours of Ekarmala as he tried to balance himself in the slush.

A lorry in front of them had its tailgate down. Logs that were beginning to get bleached jutted out of the vehicle. Morgan felt the wood.

'I have heard that the wood for the pit in which the Theyyam falls must be cut from trees in the region where the Theyyam is performed. But why are such large quantities of firewood being collected from this area and loaded onto lorries?'

'In the places you are talking about, the Ottakolam Theyyam performance happens once in fifteen or twenty-one years. In some regions, the Theechamundi Theyyam happens every three years. It's not like that in Purapuri. Here, you have a Theyyam every alternate year. If we chop down the trees that frequently, all the trees here will be lost. So Chindachchan said: Let's forget what tradition says. Let's get the wood from outside. So, wood has been coming in from other towns for three to four years now.'

Kaanaadi led the way as they struggled to walk by the sides of the parked lorries.

Little children gathered to check out the roadblock and the wood. They stared wide-eyed at Morgan, a white man slogging through ankle-deep muck. He splashed mud all around him as he walked.

'Running out of trees? How is that possible? It's trees and more trees here, whichever way you look. It's like we are in a forest.'

'True. There are many trees here. But not all trees can be chopped down to construct the *Meleri*, the fire pit. The fire that the Theyyam falls into is the fire used in the rites of Panchagni, the five fires amidst which devotees perform penance. Only the wood that can be used for the Panchagni can be used for the Meleri. Jackfruit tree, tamarind tree, champa tree—there are rules about which type of wood is to be used. A Theyyam like Pottan Theyyam, an anti-caste manifestation of Lord Shiva, requires only a small firepit. An Ottakolam, on the other hand, needs a large heap of embers for the Theyyam to run and fall in. Our local Theyyam, Irumukhan, falls into an even deeper firepit. If we were to chop down tamarind trees every other year, we would run out of trees to cut. Jackfruit trees are not a problem, we have plenty of them. It was the favourite tree of our ancestors, and we grow them in plenty. This is why Chindachchan asked us to bring trees from other regions. People accepted it because *he* said it. Had someone else made that suggestion, there would have been riots. But the first block of wood used to construct the holy fire pit is always from a tree within this town. Cutting down that block of wood is a ritual done at an auspicious time with great fanfare. For the Theyyam this year, the ritual happened yesterday at Velarkod. The last time, the wood came from Udayagiri. The *Kollikkaar* are always from the same village where the wood is sourced.

The rain had washed away most of the path they were walking on. Morgan found it hard to keep up with the much older Kaanaadi on the slippery road.

'Who are the Kollikkaar?'

'*Kolli* in these parts means firewood. The Kollikkaar are a group of people chosen to handle the wood required for the Meleri, the firepit. We call them the Kolli Committee. Along with the Theyyam performer, the Kolli committee members and four *Valikkaar*—the men who pull the Theyyam out of the firepit—go on a twenty-one-day fast. It's good that you came today. Tomorrow is the Adayalam Vaangal ceremony. The performer formally accepts betel leaves, areca nut and rice in a banana leaf as an invitation. He gets a formal communication that he is to perform the Theyyam at a particular shrine on the specified day and time. He then gets mentally and physically ready to perform the Theyyam. The vrat or the fast begins then, and after that, it may be hard to meet or talk to Chindachchan.'

Kaanaadi veered off the main road and took a narrow pathway to reach higher up the hill. It was a lovely bend with a profusion of green grass. They could see a pleasant sight: a long line of people , inching forward on foot.

When they were almost halfway up the hill, Kaanaadi pointed in the opposite direction. 'That is the Purapuri Temple.'

Morgan turned to look at a large expanse of valley floor. Right in the middle, there was a spot that looked blazing orange. He thought he was looking at fire. Once his eyes adjusted to the light, he realised it was a large yellow building. Bright sunlight on rain-soaked land played tricks on the eye.

Morgan pointed to the flat land around the temple. 'Is that Ettunaad?'

'That is Udayapuram. The other villages are located inside these mountains. That river over there is the Vannathipuzha. Beyond the river lies Velarkod.'

Kaanaadi, who was panting by then, stopped for a break. Morgan gazed at the beautiful landscape around them. He pointed to the tallest hill by the riverbank. 'Isn't that Ekarmala?'

'No, that is Ezhimala. It looks like it's close when you see it from here. Our eyes deceive us. It is very far away in reality. And despite the name, it's not Ezhimala, seven hills. There are eleven hills in total over there. Have you heard of Soorpanakha?'

'Yes, of course, the demon beauty from your stories.' Morgan's eyes were still on the temple.

'One of those hills is believed to be her cut-off breast.'

Kaanaadi began to recite lines from a much-sung song. Stray verses he had heard during Poorakkali, a festival performance in Bhagavathy temples, came to his lips. '*Ponninkasavupol minnum mula randum . . .*'

Breasts that shimmer like gold

Swaying in the wind

He recalled the tune he had forgotten and continued with full vigour. He began climbing up again.

Morgan caught up with him. 'So, where is Ekarmala?'

The song had put Kaanaadi in a playful mood. 'No matter how intensely you look in that direction, you will never find Ekarmala. Because Ekarmala is the name of the hill we are climbing right now.'

Sajith, who was part of the committee to pick out wood for the Irumukhan Theyyam, chose the lightest tree he could find. Carrying the tree to the temple, he made small talk with the committee member behind him. 'Do you know what happened the day before yesterday when we went to finalise the time to cut the trees? That scoundrel schoolteacher talked nonsense and stalled us for an hour. We had to have a bath and go back again.'

'Hmm? What happened?' The listener's voice was heavy with the effort of transporting the tree.

'Verpuli Korachchan had stepped into the room with his right leg first. The teacher said that was a bad omen. He argued with us and made us all go home, have a bath, and come back again.'

Sajith tucked his towel that had come loose to his waist. Even the smallest tree needed six people to carry it, and his legs were giving way. He imagined how hard it would be for those carrying the larger trees. The thought filled him with both sympathy and happiness.

'Isn't that a good thing? Stepping into a room with your right leg? Don't brides enter their marital home by putting the right leg forward?' The question came from someone at the back. Sajith had not yet met the committee members from the other towns, and he couldn't recognise whose voice it was. He had seen some of the guys around, but he didn't know their names.

Sajith raised his voice so he could be heard by everyone. 'After marriage, the bride comes to stay permanently at your house. The right leg is okay then. But if you are going to a house for a short while—to say something and leave immediately—then you must step in with your left leg. That's what the teacher said. How are we supposed to know all this?'

Dasan, who was right at the back, recalled the time when he had been part of the group that went to check the right time, according to astrology, to cut the trees. 'There is no point. Every year, the man raises some objection or the other.

Chindachchan didn't consult him before deciding to allow us to bring wood from outside. The teacher is miffed about that.'

By listening to the chatter of people going in and out of the house, Morgan surmised that he had arrived at Chindachchan's house. The house wasn't as far as he had expected it to be. The appearance of the house, too, was not how he had imagined it would be. Though not a tall building, the house was in the style of a large Naalukettu. The carvings and woodwork were not as elaborate as the traditional old houses of the region, but the size of the house surprised Morgan.

Chindachchan was watering the plants, mostly saplings, in the yard. A few shirtless men gave him fresh pots of water as he went around the garden. There was a long queue of people waiting patiently to meet him. Morgan tried to get behind the queue, but Kaanaadi pulled him away. Kaanaadi pointed out who Chindachchan was. Chindachchan stood out in the crowd with the sculpted body of a performing artist.

Chindachchan was exchanging pleasantries with those waiting to see him and tending to his plants at the same time. He was like a glowing deepasthambam, the large multi-tiered lamp that can hold hundreds of wicks at the same time.

Morgan looked at him, unblinking. As soon as he saw Morgan, Chindachchan gave his pot of water to an aide and walked towards him. Morgan took a few long strides to reach him.

'All that walking must have been a bother?'

Morgan wasn't expecting such a soft voice from that muscular frame. He couldn't find the words to respond. He felt as if he was facing a mesmerising presence. Chindachchan began to ask him something, but suddenly there was a commotion. A noisy group of men with mundus folded up to their knees and wearing black triangular waistbands walked in. The group split into two to make way for five men. Morgan recognised them. They were the select group of men chosen to assist the temple priest at the Theyyam venue. Like the rest of the crowd, he moved backwards to give them space.

Like the hundreds of visitors who had come to meet Chindachchan, Morgan, too, sat down for a meal in the long dining room attached to the house. He ate poha, plantain, and a kheer made of puffed rice. Kaanaadi asked for idli and piping hot sambhar. He introduced Morgan to a young boy who was serving dry coconut chutney from a steel pot. 'This is Chindachchan's son.' The boy looked flustered and served Morgan some chutney even though it didn't go with the dish Morgan had asked for.

'Forgive me for asking this, but based on what I've read, Theyyam artists normally live in poverty. How does Chindachchan manage to live in such luxury?' Morgan lowered his voice, unsure if he was being inappropriate.

Kaanaadi tore off a large piece of idli and dunked it in sambhar. 'This temple follows a practice that no other temple in the world does. When there is an Irumukhan Theyyam performance at the temple, all the donations collected in the temple hundi go to the performer. Sometimes, the donation box receives gold bars that are too heavy to lift. A lot of people from all over the world come to see the Theyyam here. Even collections from people who come only to pray are enough to fill three long mundus.'

Morgan savoured the sickly sweet payasam that he was eating for the first time. 'That's good, right? If these people prosper, then other people in the town, too, will benefit.'

Kaanaadi laughed. 'Temporarily, yes. If you keep the purse strings tight, it will travel through generations. But inherited wealth makes people selfish and evil. Chindachchan knows that and probably that's why he spends money so lavishly. His father was an even better man.'

The room arranged for Morgan in the house was a curious one. At the end of the house, there was a long corridor that led to a series of stone steps. If you climbed down the steps, you would reach a square paddy threshing ground. To the right was a long room. The room itself was ordinary. But the view of the valley and the temple from the edge of the threshing ground was spectacular. Much grander and vaster than Morgan had imagined it would be after his first glimpse. Even though it was a tough climb up the steps to reach the main house, the sight of the temple cooled his eyes and soul. When moonlight spread its hood in the night, the place looked even more beautiful. Though he was exhausted after long days of travel, Morgan spent some time enjoying the beauty of the valley. It was quite late when he hit the bed.

He was still sleeping when Kaanaadi knocked on his door. Chindachchan had sent for him. He had a quick wash. Outside, the intensity of the sun indicated it was close to noon. The rain clouds had disappeared, and the day was bright and humid. When he rushed to the steps of the veranda, Chindachchan looked like he was all set to go on a journey. He had a cloth bag on his shoulder.

Chindachchan touched the feet of everyone present there, including women and children. He stepped closer to Morgan and bowed low like a ripe paddy stalk to touch his feet. Morgan, who didn't expect that gesture, was stupefied. He bent down, held Chindachchan's shoulders and helped him up.

Chindachchan's expression remained unchanged as he moved on to the next person, a man supported by crutches. Tears streamed down the man's face as Chindachchan looked into his eyes.

Even after Chindachchan had left, the plants were not neglected. There was no noise and crowds like on the previous day. Three boys struggled to carry water in pots. Morgan recognised one of them as Chindachchan's son. A hefty man took the pots from the boys and watered the plants.

The man without legs, whom he had seen in the morning, stood by, giving instructions. Morgan wondered why they were drawing water from the well, taking so much trouble to source water during the monsoon.

'That is Kodumudi. Kannagi's younger brother. Kannagi was Chindachchan's wife … Didn't we see that Tamil Nadu lorry yesterday? Kodumudi drove it here. He will be here until the Theyyam is over and Chindachchan regains his health. The other fellow is Kelan. He is my brother.'

Morgan was so immersed in the scenes in the yard that he was startled when he heard Kaanaadi's voice. He had not noticed Kaanaadi approaching him.

'What happened to his legs?'

'An accident during a Theyyam. The Ottakolam Theyyam wears something called the Arayoda that comes right up to his waist. It is made of green coconut palms.' Kaanaadi began to explain with gestures.

'I know that. I have seen it on the body of Vishnumoorthy Theyyam.'

Kaanaadi was taken aback by this piece of information.

'Oh, okay. So, this Arayoda is what shields the performer's body from burns when he falls into the heap of embers. Towards the end of the performance, the Theyyam removes the Arayoda and jumps into the fire. But only for a few moments. At this point, the performer will be covered with coconut fronds only below the waist. He will also be holding some coconut fronds in his hand. The area above the waist is vulnerable. It is a dangerous game. So, when the Theyyam performer jumps into the fire, what saves him is the skill of the Valikkaar, the attendants who pull him away with ropes. The two attendants and the Theyyam must be of one body in those moments. If the performer or the attendants hesitate for a second, if they feel any fear or if they put the wrong foot forward, the Theyyam will be roasted on the fire like a poppadom. After this, the Theyyam sits down in the Meleri, the firepit. At this point, the attendants must be as fast as a lightning bolt. He should be brought up as soon as he sits. You cannot lift the Theyyam with a rope. Normally, when you pull up the Theyyam from the firepit, he slips through the embers to the ground. When he hits the ground, four people lift him. But in this case, he is sitting on the Meleri. You cannot drag him down because he is sitting. You need to hold his hand and bring him up like you would help a person who is sitting on the floor get up. If you pull the rope from below, you will not get the required thrust. By then, the Theyyam would be like a living corpse. He will be heavier. You must get on to the embers and pull him up. The attendants' feet are bound to scorch and swell up. So, we have a trick for that. The Theyyam might sit on the Meleri suddenly. So, the palm fronds round his waist will fan out around him, the way a girl's flared dress might create a circle around her. The attendants target the coconut leaves when they jump onto the Meleri. Their feet should hit the palm fronds. The young leaves might have dried up by then. Nonetheless, the leaves create a cushion between the attendants' feet and blazing embers. So, the attendants stamp on the Meleri with full force, and the embers swing back. That force helps them get the performer to his feet.

'When Kelan was a Valikkaaran one time, the palm fronds didn't spread out. That wasn't an Irumukhan Theyyam performance. It was an Ottakolam in Payyannur. Irumukhan does not remove his Arayoda. It is not part of the performance. After jumping into the fire, Irumukhan falls into a bed of thorns.

'Kelan had to act instantly. After stepping on the embers, he decided to pull the Theyyam back and lift him. There was no time to think. If he hesitated, the other attendant would lose his footing. Even otherwise, just touching or stamping on embers doesn't burn you if you have enough mental strength and presence of mind. There is a ritual where the Kollikkaar, the wood committee I told you about, jump onto the Meleri and run to the other side of the arena. They don't get hurt. It's a question of how strong your mind is. The Kollikkaar are on the embers for an instant and then they dash to the other side. It is not the same with Valikkaar, the attendants. When the wood turns to embers, the earth around is red hot too. Sometimes, the ground is even hotter than fire. If the Theyyam falls into the fire a hundred and one times, the attendants will pull him away from this ground each time. So, their feet are damaged in any case. Call it Kelan's luck. When he jumped into the embers, his feet sank in. The other attendants pulled him back but the damage was done. It looked like a small burn then. He managed for two years. Chindachchan spent a lot of money on Kelan's treatment, but there was no use. The infection spread upwards, and his legs had to be amputated.'

Kaanaadi gasped at the memory. Morgan looked at Kelan and shivered. A gaunt, bent figure with wooden crutches under his arms. His face was a face full of stories. Morgan gazed at him and imagined a Theyyam. The *Mudi*, the crown, was gone, but it seemed like nothing could erase the Mukhamezhuthu colours from his face. His face had deep lines. As if time had etched all the burning paths the man had walked in his lifetime on his countenance.

Everyone, including little children, stood up when Chindachchan came in for the Adayalam ritual. They cheered when he walked out with betel leaf and areca nut.

Not everyone was happy, though. Achchan Namboodiri later vented his frustration before his sidekick Kangaani. 'People got into a tizzy as if the ocean was being churned. Chindan was below the steps. I walked up and sat on top of the steps. And yet, apart from a few village elders, no one showed me any respect. This is not a new thing. It's become the norm. I have heard that the temple was built from the wealth donated by this house, my ancestral home. If I look for the title deed of this house, many of those cheering for Chindan will be indebted to this house. But we no longer have any value in this town, Kangaani!'

Achchan Namboodiri flung the open tender coconut that he had been given to drink.

'You know, Kangaani, even the women are now drawn to him.'

The coconut bounced off the raised Tulsi plant platform and landed in slushy water. The sight of the coconut spinning in the dirty water increased Namboodiri's urge for vengeance.

'That is true. Right in front of our eyes, he has been growing unchecked. Had we cut off his branch right at the beginning, he would have been restrained by the shade we provide. Seen how tall he has grown? There is no point in pruning his branches now. The tree must be destroyed from its roots.'

The hatred in Kangaani's voice delighted Achchan Namboodiri. He spat into a puddle of rainwater. 'Is there any axe strong enough to chop off that tree in Ettunaad today, Kangaani?'

'It's not enough if the iron is sharp. An axe needs to be held at the right angle if it is to be used as a weapon. If the weapon is not used correctly, it harms the one wielding it. To cut a tree, you need the help of another tree. Someone from his own tribe. What is the best stand for an axe, Nambooricha? Isn't it the tree itself?' Kangaani laughed, doing a crude mimicry of the Theyyam.

He cut off the head of another tender coconut with a cleaver and handed it over to Namboodiri. He felt it was inauspicious to delay the execution of a good idea. So, he set out immediately.

There was a huge pavilion being erected in front of the temple. Giri was creating channels around the pavilion so that rainwater would not enter the pandals. Kangaani called out to him and led him to a fig tree. 'Do you want to be their minion for all time, Giri?'

Kangaani sat down on the stone enclosure around the tree and asked Giri to join him. 'Your father Kelu Panikkar and I go back a long way. We have known each other since we were little. Once, when I was bitten by a snake in Peelimudi, your father was the one whom I literally leant against. He propped me up and walked with me for a long distance to ensure I got the anti-venom from the poison devil tree. He stayed with me until I got better. He is a boor, which is why he never lets me express the gratitude and affection I feel for him. And when I see you—Kelu Panikkar's son—get by like this, it hurts me. Even though you walk behind Chindan like a shadow, I know your heart is not in it. I know what your great desire is.' Kangaani paused, waiting to see how Giri would respond.

Giri thought Kangaani was talking about the woman he loved, Praseetha. So he sat coyly, not uttering a word.

'I know your real ambition is to get a job in the Gulf. A few offers almost came through. But that is a foreign land. If we don't have someone living there to guide us, we could get duped. That is why I didn't speak up earlier. But now, things are different. You know Achchan Namboodiri's eldest son, Anand? He is there now. I have arranged a job for you with his help. You have nothing to worry about because he is there. After this Theyyam, you can get into that country. Just be mentally prepared for that.'

Before Giri could answer, Kangaani walked away.

On the veranda of Chindachchan's house, Morgan stood admiring a painting of the Irumukhan. He was most interested in the intricacies of the Mukhamezhuthu, the face paint, of the Theyyam. 'Tell me, what's the real story behind this Theyyam?' he asked Kaanaadi.

'Each Theyyam has many legends and folktales associated with it. Even Irumukhan has a story. When you go to the temple near here, there is a palatial house by the temple pool. It is the house of one Achchan Namboodiri. You could say that they were the feudal lords here. I will show you the house when we pass by the temple. They are the traditional Thantris of this place, the ones who set rules in the temples.

'A few generations ago, Achchan Namboodiri had an ancestor called Venadhiri. The cowherd who looked after his cattle was a young man named Kunki. In those days, many felt that Kunki was Venadhiri's son from one of his concubines. Peelimudi was then an impenetrable forest. Stories of tigers entering the villages and making off with cattle were common. One day, a tiger destroyed Venadhiri's cattle shed and killed a cow. Venadhiri sent Kunki into the deep forest to kill the tiger. He saw this as a golden opportunity to get rid of Kunki. That was the time when Lord Shiva and Parvathy had decided to spend a few days in Peelimudi in the disguise of a pair of tigers.

'Kunki hadn't even killed a hen before, but his arrow hit the mark on that day. Eight young people, each from the eight houses surrounding the forest, had accompanied Kunki on his mission. Their descendants are today the residents of Ettunaad village.

'Lord Shiva had transferred his powers to his son Vairajathan at Mount Kailasa and was living the life of an ordinary animal in the Peelimudi forest at the time. He thought that the tiger Kunki had killed was Parvathy. So, in the form of a tiger, Lord Shiva clawed the flesh off Kunki's body.

'It is to evoke the memory of this incident that the Theyyam rolls on a bed of thorny thistles and gets himself bleeding.

'Pressure from his wife led Venadhiri to send his army chief Vallyedathu Nair in search of Kunki. When Nair entered the forest, he saw the dead tiger. To make it seem as if he had killed the tiger, Vallyedathu lit a fire and killed the flailing Kunki. One legend says that Irumukhan climbs into the Meleri pit in memory of this event.

'Some versions of the story state that Nair reached Venadhiri's Illam, his large traditional house, with the dead tiger. And when Kunki's wife, Naani, came in search of Venadhiri, the feudal lords killed Naani with an axe. When Lord Shiva found out about this, he sent Vairajathan to the scene. Vairajathan killed Nair and Venadhiri and hung them up on a pole. The story goes that Venadhiri's home, with its eight halls and two central courtyards, was razed to the ground. This blaze is symbolised by a particular act in Theyyam in which attendants step onto the heap of embers and walk to the other side of the arena. That's what some people believe. In any case, Vairajathan raised Kunki to the status of a god. This valiant form of the Deivam, the god, is Irumukhan Theyyam. In the monsoon season, the performance of Irumukhan alone happens outside the walls of the temple. During the Kaliyaattam, when the grand Theyyam performances happen inside the temple in December, a dance is performed in Naani's name.' Kaanaadi pointed to a black and white photograph hung on the wall to illustrate his story.

'There are some changes in the story you narrated,' said Sukumaran Nair, a temple committee member. He had come in to get a change of clothes for Chindachchan, and was now sitting on the veranda, drinking a glass of tea and listening to Kaanaadi's story.

'Their Theyyam stories never stand to reason or common sense. Lord Shiva came to the forest in the form of a tiger and knew nothing of what was happening, it seems! These tales are good enough for their level. But none of it is true. Forget everything else, it was Vallyedathu Nair who killed the tiger that day. If Kunki set his mind to it, he could probably kill a mosquito. He could not go beyond that. You know he was incapable just by hearing the name Kunki! To kill a tiger, you need a good Nair. That has been the case, then and now.'

'Vallyedathu Nair wasn't the godfather of the Nair community, as you seem to think. Nair in these parts only means that he was the chief of the militia of the then feudal lord.' Kaanaadi's voice was sharp and barely hid his sarcasm.

The Lion's Tale - 2

'After this Theyyam, Chindan will become just another forgotten fable. Maybe a ludicrous figure for the children to laugh at when they play Kolkali. Despite being born in the modern age, I can fight a battle like my ancestors did. I never dreamt I would get this opportunity.' Achchan Namboodiri rubbed his hands in glee.

Giridharan was seated on the table, fists clenched, his head bent over. Namboodiri could sense from his body language that Giri wasn't too interested in the plan. He pulled up a chair and sat closer to Giri.

'Giri, I will tell you an old story. I can't call it a story, really. It's something that happened when you were little. I was a witness. You were a little boy. During the Kaliyaattam, tender coconut vendors would line up to do business at Vadakkeppuram. When you saw them, you instantly felt the urge to have a tender coconut. Not for the water, but for the smooth white flesh of the young coconut. You led your father, Kelu Panikkar, to the vendors. This fellow was also a kid then,' Achchan Namboodiri said, gesturing towards Kangaani.

'Kelu did not have the money to buy that tender coconut. He hesitated, upset that he could not fulfil his son's small wish. You will understand his state of mind only when you have your own child. I don't remember how much a tender coconut cost back then. But Kelu only had half that amount in his pocket. He quietly asked a vendor if he could give him a small coconut at that price.

'The seller picked the smallest fruit from his stock and shaved the top open. You forced your father to drink the water, and then asked the vendor to split the coconut open. Kelu almost fainted. The inside was empty. That coconut only had water. You threw a fit, rolling in the mud and crying out loud. The vendors began to mock Kelu. The villagers standing around all smirked, suppressing their laughter.

'When I talk about this now, it seems like a trivial incident. But I know the depth of the wound that Kelu and you suffered that day, Giri. When you have a child tomorrow, that child shouldn't face the same situation. Our insatiable wants and needs turn us towards the gods. But those gods are only stand-ins. The real god, Giri, is money.' Namboodiri stroked Giri's arm.

On an evening when the rain took a break, Morgan and Kaanaadi set out for a little trip. Even though it had been four days since he reached Ettunaad, Morgan still hadn't visited the temple. When he arrived, Morgan had planned to explore the town and temple the next day. But he wasn't in the mood for anything once he settled in. The stay at Chindachchan's house was comfortable. He hadn't ever experienced this kind of peace, and his mind seemed very relaxed.

'Kaanaadi, don't you play the Theyyam?'

Kaanaadi curled his left palm to make a hollow. He placed a leaf of the Thoovali he had picked from the ground inside the hollow. He looked up at Morgan. 'What kind of a question is that, sir? Had I played the Theyyam, would I have been alive for so long?' He laughed. 'Theyyam performers grow old really quickly. Aren't I still full of beans?' With his right hand, Kaanaadi burst the Thoovali leaf as if it were a cracker.

'When Chindachchan said a Sayippu was coming to see the Theyyam, I got flustered. I trained myself in sign language before I came to see you. But the way you speak Malayalam, sir … us Malayalis should bow our heads down before you. There is no trace of an accent. By any chance, were you born and raised here? Why are you here? Please don't be offended at my asking this … I am truly curious.' Kaanaadi slowed down so that Morgan could catch up with him.

Morgan smiled. 'I speak seventeen languages in total. As a child, I was like our Kodumudi. I was mute. I started speaking very late. Now, I am talking too much, almost as if I am making up for my initial silence with interest.'

They sauntered along, relishing every little sight on their way. The luxuriant rain had made everything look plump and clear. The Vannathipuzha was overflowing its banks after heavy showers in the eastern districts. They enjoyed the river's new muddy brown hue.

'I am doing a study on the use of masks in art forms across the world. Even after coming to India, and then to Kerala, it took me a long time to reach Theyyam. The face painting in

Theyyam is also a kind of mask, isn't it? At first, I was simply stunned by the beauty of the Mukhamezhuthu. This style of painting has the power to instantly arrest the attention of anyone who looks at the Theyyam. I was aware, in theory, of the details and intricacies of this style.

'But the first time I saw how the face was painted, I was shocked. The drawing is done upside down. I had pictured the painter sitting in front of the performer and painting his face. But what I saw instead was the Theyyam lying down, and the artist seated facing his head. From the perspective of the artist, his subject's face is upside down. I was blown away. From that moment on, I began to yearn to learn more about Theyyam.'

Morgan walked to the river and washed his hands and face, caring little for how muddy the water was.

It was dusk when they reached the temple. The stabs of light emanating from the hundreds of lamps lit around the temple enclosure lent a shine to the surroundings. From outside, it seemed to Morgan as if flames were flying. They looked like glowworms in the dark.

The workers were still sawing branches off trees and stacking up the wood. After spending some time there, Morgan returned to his temporary home. He wanted to see more of the temple, but it was too late by then.

In the past ten days, Morgan had become aware that Chindachchan's house, 'Kishkinda', was almost like a pilgrimage shrine. Flocks of people walked in and out, many of them patients. Everyone who came always said they ate the tastiest meals there. They were sent to the dining hall after their problems were solved. Or at least, they felt they had been heard.

In his short time there, Morgan recognised that ninety-nine per cent of poor people's problems could be sorted out with money.

❧

When Kangaani slowed down the Jeep to avoid the slush on the road, Achchan Namboodiri noticed that one of the pedestrians in front of them was Kaanaadi.

'Ah! Is it you, Kaanaadi? If you're going downhill, get in. We will drop you.' Namboodiri stared at Kaanaadi's companion as he invited them into his Jeep.

Giridharan opened the back door to let them in. Kaanaadi recalled the local gossip that Giri had been spending almost all his time with Achchan Namboodiri of late. Giri placed his right hand on his chest and nodded, a sign of respect.

Achchan Namboodiri nudged Kangaani, directing him to start driving. 'The roof tiles of the school are broken in some parts. The schoolmaster has been complaining for some days now. Now that it's Theyyam season, the Master will mostly be at the temple, busy with astrological calculations and other things. He will keep whining about this. That is why we went to the temple. Turned out to be a good thing. The leaks are more severe than I thought. We need to call someone at the earliest to repair the roof. By the way, what are you both doing on this route?'

'We went to the school too, to drop off Chindachchan's kids. We saw your Jeep there.'

Kangaani glanced at Kaanaadi in the rear-view mirror.

'This is Morgan. He has come to see the Theyyam here. He is staying at Chindachchan's house,' said Kaanaadi. Namboodiri turned around and smiled at Morgan.

'Didn't I tell you the other day about a Namboodiri who lives in a house near the temple? This is him. And the school where Aadi and the rest study—that's his too.' Kaanaadi filled Morgan in after they got off the Jeep. But he was full of doubts. Why would Giri spend so much time with Namboodiri at a time when he was on a fast? He had heard about their sudden friendship, but now he had witnessed the camaraderie. Namboodiri was a person who wouldn't even move a dry leaf if it didn't benefit him. The more Kaanaadi thought about it, the heavier his heart felt.

The days slipped away, as silently and swiftly as oil from a lamp. It was only when Giri came to pluck flowers that Morgan realised it was the day when logs would be stacked for the Meleri. Morgan tried to make small talk with Giri because they had met before, but Giri stayed aloof.

Kaanaadi came looking for Giri. 'Why are you plucking the ixora flowers from the garden?'

'Don't I need it for the headgear and the facial makeup? The work on the palm leaves and the waistband is almost over. Why are you not coming to the Sacred Grove? Everyone there is asking about Kaanaadi Achchan.'

Giri picked the flowers at lightning speed and put them into a basket made of palm leaves.

'If you use this flower to make the *Kambi*, the man will die when he hits the embers. To protect him, you need to get the wild ixora flowers, not the ones we grow in the garden. You have to go to Peelimudi. I will come with you. Why would you pick flowers from this garden … it's not the first time you are doing this.'

Giri put his basket down. He gave Kaanaadi a piercing stare and made his way out through the bushes. Kaanaadi emptied the basket of flowers and gave it to Morgan. They didn't walk far. Kaanaadi knew the exact spot where wild ixoras grew in Peelimudi. Years of practice had given him the same speed and dexterity as Giri to pick the flowers. Morgan watched as the basket filled quickly with red flowers.

'You can only use flowers that grow on the rocks to make the Kambi. Giri has so much experience and knowledge, but he seems to be going backwards. This is an important step. Once the Theyyam falls into the smouldering pit, he cannot back out even if he wants to. Even if his mind says no, he must keep jumping into the Meleri continuously, so long as the attendants keep pulling him back. No one stops the Theyyam until he falls into the fire at least a hundred and one times. Even if there is danger, no one can do anything then. The only time we can do something is now. Every step has to be executed with zero error.'

Kaanaadi held on to a creeper hanging loose on the rock and climbed up. Morgan tried to do the same, but he slipped down the rock and fell. When he tried to climb up again, his knees hit the rock. Kaanaadi jumped among the creepers with the agility of a monkey. Only when he lent a hand could Morgan climb up.

'What is the meaning of "Kambi"?'

'Kambi is the most important ornament adorning the Theyyam above the neck. It is tied to both the ears. There are other ornaments too: *Thalappaali, Thanda, Peeli, Kondal* and *Thalappoo*. These are there for aesthetic reasons. But the Kambi's purpose is different. We believe that heat and cold enter the body through the ears. The Kambi is tied to prevent the heat of the Meleri from entering the Theyyam's brain through his ears. People say the Theyyam feels a cool breeze when he sees the glowing embers. There is no limit to the nonsense people can say. Only we know the reality. Honestly, a performer must be mindful of everything, including the direction of the wind. So,, people can spout any sort of nonsense, but the truth is, we are literally playing with fire here. You can't be too careful.' Kaanaadi let out a deep sigh.

When Kaanaadi and Morgan returned to the temple, the ritual of stacking firewood for the firepit was halfway through. Logs of wood were piled up, one on top of the other. The pile was so high that Morgan thought the work of assembling the wood was over. He was utterly disappointed that he could not watch the ceremony from the beginning. But it turned out that there was a long way to go.

Six or seven young men wearing towels around their waists had climbed onto the mountain of wood and were hauling up more logs. Their helpers stood precariously at various levels of the heap, passing logs to the men above them. Morgan watched them with apprehension. If even a few logs upset the balance, the whole pile of wood would come crashing down on these men. The possibility of an accident was high.

The men had no harness, no protective gear, as they climbed higher and higher with logs of wood. The process of making sure that the wood found its right place on top of the pile was harder than passing up the wood from down below.

As Morgan watched, a log of wood slid down the pile. A gasp from the crowd alerted the young man who was wielding the axe on the wood below. Fortunately for him, the log that fell was a light piece of firewood, and he escaped unharmed.

As the mound of wood gained height, the heavy logs gave way to lighter kindling woven into a spiral. Experienced men gave directions, but none of them were allowed to touch the wood or help the committee of youth who had been chosen to build the Meleri.

As the pile got higher, the number of people on top of the mound became smaller. The pace of work slowed down. Sending logs to the top became a job that required great focus. Each of the young men's movements reflected their attention to detail and precision. It was as if they were constructing a house of cards. Finally, there were only two people on top of the mound.

When his neck began to strain from the effort of looking up, Morgan walked away from the logs. He found a spot at a distance from where he could sit and watch the action. From his vantage point, the two people on top now looked like ants.

The pile of wood stood strong in front of the temple like Ravana's fort, almost three times higher than the main entrance of the temple.

Morgan struggled to imagine the amount of heat that would be generated by burning all this wood. He watched the workers complete their tasks. They gathered palm leaves to start the fire and then went to take a dip in the temple pool.

Kaanaadi urged him to eat at the temple, but Morgan hesitated. He went back to Chindachchan's home, where Kannagi had cooked dinner for him. After a meal and shower, he returned to the temple along with Aadi. Saravanan and Anand had set out earlier with Kelan.

Morgan reached there at the right time. The village elders, the temple trustees and administrators were going around the mountain of wood. They were led by Kaatti, the official lighter of lamps at the temple. Kaatti had a banana leaf in his hand with lighted wicks on its ends. This was called the Kodiyila. The people following Kaatti threw grains of rice and something that looked like raw turmeric in the direction of the logs. Most of them were elderly men. Some young men had long towels tied around their waists, and they were wielding the symbolic mace.

After they ceremoniously went around the Meleri thrice, Kaatti bowed down and placed the blazing Kodiyila at the foot of the mound. The eight village elders came forward, each with an unlit torch made with a thin bundle of dried coconut palms. They lit their torches and stood in eight directions around the wood. Then, together they set fire to the Meleri.

The bottom of the mound began to spark. White smoke rose from the top of the pile where the fire had yet to make its mark. The fire slowly began to spread upwards.

The Lion's Tale - 3

'Ah-aha! You are here? Come down. Chindachchan has been looking for you.' Kaanaadi finally found Morgan after making inquiries and walking through a noisy crowd.

After the offerings to the deity, the village elders came to announce the time for the first ritual. Chindachchan had asked for Morgan then. Kaanaadi and Morgan squeezed through the crowd and somehow crossed the temple gate. The rituals had already begun in the chamber. Chindachchan had draped a white cloth over the red garment he was wearing. A piece of the garment opened out like a long fan behind him. It resisted the wind like a ship's taut mast and swayed rhythmically with Chindan's movements. There were no lines or paint on his face yet. But the aura created by that majestic red fabric radiated grandeur.

After a few offerings and rituals, Kaatti came out of the temple with a banana leaf with lighted wicks on it, like the Kodiyila used to light the holy firepit. Chindachchan accepted a few grains of rice from Kaatti's left palm and scattered some in the air, and then on the leaf. With reverence, he accepted the flaming banana leaf.

The loud beats of the Asura Taal on the Chenda were drowned out by the ear-splitting sound of firecrackers outside. Chindachchan circled the Kodiyila clockwise and bowed to the crowd.

When the sounds of the crackers faded, Morgan turned to Kaanaadi: 'I see the burning wicks. But what else is there on that banana leaf?'

'Nothing special. Arecanut, betel leaf, turmeric, grains of rice. The wicks on the Kodiyila are lit in the inner chamber of the temple. The idea is to invoke the power and persona of the god in the Kodiyila. That divinity is in turn passed on to the Theyyam performer when he receives the banana leaf.'

After the Thedangal, the first ritual, Chindachchan stood up for the Thottam, a performance with ballads before the Theyyam. Skyrockets hummed in the air at random intervals. Below the waist, the costume of the Thottam was like the flared, starched skirts worn by Kathakali dancers. Strings of garland were woven tightly around his chest. But the lack of face paint was still a disappointment to Morgan.

The Thottam came out and tried to jump into the firepit. The wood committee members rushed to stop him. They grabbed him, brought him under control, and took him inside the temple. This time, too, the Thottam received the Kodiyila and bowed to the audience from all directions. Morgan felt that the piercing gaze of the Thottam was fixed on a dimension far beyond the audience.

Kaanaadi whispered into Morgan's ears: 'He is worshipping the guardians of the directions. We believe that eight deities rule specific directions of space: Indran, Agni, Yaman, Niruthi, Varunan, Vayu, Kuberan and Ishana.' As the drumbeats rose, the performer's feet moved in quick, mesmerising steps. In a language that sounded ancient to Morgan, the Theyyam shouted battle cries. He guffawed and made guttural sounds that resembled the cries of animals.

Morgan looked at Chindachchan's unpainted face, towering above the costume of the Thottam. The lack of Mukhamezhuthu, the face paint, was a drawback, but it was not a mistake. The torch lit up the red crown on Chindachchan's head. Underneath that, Chindachchan's regal face shone like the sun. When he was armed, Chindachchan went close to the Meleri again. The heap of logs crackled and roared. He raised his weapons, reflecting tongues of flame from the raging fire, and walked around the pit.

'This ritual serves another purpose. When he circles around the fire, the Theyyam is able to gauge the heat and height of the Meleri.' Morgan had now climbed a wall to get a better view. He was listening to every word Kaanaadi was saying.

The Theyyam made a few offerings. A bunch of spent hens was slaughtered as a sacrifice. The warrior-like dance moves of the Theyyam made the crowd shudder. Some of the steps, Morgan thought, went beyond Kalaripayattu. It was late in the night when Chindachchan finished the Thottam's performance.

The temple emptied out quite a bit after that. Only a few people hung around the premises. Volunteers, umbrella-holders, trustees, people seeking solitude, and energetic children who didn't want to go to bed. Even outside, only the wood committee members stood around the Meleri to check on the flames.

Kaanaadi showed Morgan a garment made of shiny palm leaves. 'This is the Arayoda, the waist dress. Didn't I tell you about this the other day? The Theyyam has to hold his arms up when they tie this right below his chest.'

The Arayoda, Morgan observed, had been made by splitting the tender leaves of coconut palm and weaving them together. Probably, the leaves protected the Theyyam when he fell onto the red-hot embers. He had once seen the same garment on a Vishnumoorthy Theyyam. He tried to lift up the Arayoda but failed. He mustered some more strength and tried again. No luck. 'This is quite heavy!'

Kaanaadi straightened out a stray leaf. 'About fifty kilograms, possibly. When you tie it, you feel a tightness around your waist. Almost as if your spine is about to split. Chindachchan says you experience pins and needles. Only the strongest men can wear this. If you are weak in body and spirit, you might tumble backwards.'

Morgan looked at the garment in awe. 'But doesn't it offer the performer protection from fire?'

'That's true. But every time the Theyyam falls into the bed of embers, his chest hits hard against this garment. Makes it difficult to breathe,' Kaanaadi sighed.

He turned his attention to a pretty round headdress. 'This is the Mudi, or crown, of a Theyyam called Kshetrapalakan. Literally, the one who protects the temple. Tomorrow, you will witness a performance of this Theyyam too, along with Irumukhan's.'

After removing the Thottam costume, Chindachchan set out for a bath and a meal. He also needed to finish some rituals by dawn. The temple premises emptied out even further. After he left, Kaanaadi leaned back against the palm walls of the green room and dozed off.

Morgan spent some time roaming around the empty temple halls. He stood by the Meleri for a while. The giant pile of firewood had been burning for hours, but it did not break or crumble. You could still see the red-hot wood through the flames.

Morgan returned to the green room. Chindachchan was lying down for the Mukhamezhuthu. He had stretched himself flat before the artist and fallen asleep. Morgan knew that the Theyyam had very limited time to rest, and he did not want to cause any disturbance. So, he quietly sat down next to the artist.

The lines and patterns were similar to that of Vishnumoorthy theyyam. Swirls on either side of the cheek. A Sudarshana on the forehead. Kozhi Pushpam, denoting the comb of a rooster, on both sides of the nose. Morgan observed the beautiful Kozhi Pushpam. He understood that there was a deep, unbreakable connection between the Theyyam and the rooster.

The eyes, he noticed, were not painted in the style of a Vishnumoorthy. The thick eyebrows used to accentuate the intensity of Vishnumoorthy's eyes were absent here. Instead, the pattern around the eyes was a crab motif normally seen in the Raktha Chamundi theyyam.

Kaanaadi had woken up by now. 'The lines around the eyes are drawn carefully. The attention to detail here will impact the whole look of the Theyyam. But this beauty is short-lived. However lovely the paint, it all turns into soot when the Theyyam jumps onto the embers.'

The artist finished his work and stood up. The three of them left the room, leaving Chindachchan to his slumber.

'This is my son, Sachin,' Kaanaadi introduced the artist to Morgan.

Outside, a huge crowd had assembled in front of the Meleri. People woke up before dawn and headed to the temple, eager to see the Theyyam. The pile of logs had burned and was now a heap of embers as tall as two men. The wood committee members had split into groups of four. They were inspecting the embers, prodding the heap with long branches.

'Some stubborn twigs get left behind. The ones that don't fully turn into embers—they are picking those out. If they don't do that, when the Theyyam falls, one part of the firepit sinks while embers from the other side scatter into the air. If an ember enters the Theyyam's garment, it can be taken out only after the performance,' Sachin explained.

The committee members braved the embers, though the intense heat sometimes sent them rushing away from the fire. Forget standing near the firepit, it was hard to even look at the smouldering embers. But every visitor first came to the Meleri before going inside the temple.

'In a while, there will be a ritual where the team that worked on the Meleri will come running to jump on these embers. If we stay here, we can see that. If we go in, we can see the Theyyam getting dressed. What do you want to do?' Kaanaadi gave Morgan a choice.

'Let's go down. I want to see the costumes and ornaments.' Morgan followed Sachin to the green room.

When they got there, the first layer of the garment was being tied around Chindachchan's waist. The attendant tightened a string around his chest and asked: 'Too tight?' Chindachchan shook his head. Each attendant tugged at the string from various directions and asked him the same question. Chindachchan gave the same response: a shake of the head to signal 'no'.

'Why doesn't he answer?' Morgan whispered into Kaanaadi's ear.

Kaanaadi spoke in a low voice. 'Is this a question that needs an answer? Any discomfort? The answer to that is there is always discomfort. There is only discomfort. But the performer can't say anything. The strength of the rope that the attendants use to pull the Theyyam out of the firepit rests on that string around his waist. They tie it snugly. The tightness does not depend on the performer's comfort alone, but also on the comfort of the attendants. They ask the question as part of the ritual.'

Above the Theyyam's neck, there was a whole lot of ornaments and paraphernalia. Morgan could not recognise Chindachchan under all that face paint.

'Let's try to raise him up,' Giri told the costumiers. They held up the Theyyam from four directions with the ropes, lifted him up in the air, and brought him down.

'Not enough. Raise your arms up as high as you can and then bring him down,' Kaanaadi instructed.

The next time, they raised the Theyyam as high up as possible and suspended him in the air for a while.

Chindachchan moved his face from side to side. That was a fearsome sight. When Giri shouted out a cue, they all brought Chindachchan down to his feet. Five to six rounds of practice followed. Only then was Chindachchan led out of the green room.

When he came out, Chindachchan was mobbed. The Kollikkaar were sweeping stray bits of charred wood back into the Meleri. They held up strings of pleated palm leaves as a shield against the heat.

The Theyyam received the Kodiyila from the inner chamber of the temple, and then walked to the firepit with an attendant. The Ettunaad army stood on either side of their path, hands raised in the air. After circumambulating with Chindachchan around the heap of embers, the attendant picked up an ember from the Meleri and placed it on the Kodiyila. Chindachchan the Theyyam returned to the temple's inner chamber with the ember and the burning wicks on the Kodiyila.

The premises were overrun by a sea of humanity by then. As he looked at the crowd, Morgan wondered how such a large number of people could squeeze into such cramped spaces. Curls of smoke rose whimsically from the pile of burning wood, which was red hot by now. Morgan lacked the courage to look at the firepit for too long.

He returned to the spot where the finishing touches were being added to Chindachchan's costume and makeup. The dressers were applying a thick, white, gum-like paste to his chest. Then they put thick red-coloured cloth gloves on his hands.

Lines set to the beat of the Thottam ballads and the rhythm of the drums lent a primal, energy to the atmosphere. Two people carried the waist dress, the Arayoda, to the room. Chindachchan the Theyyam raised his hands, and the dressers wrapped the garment around his body. Chindachchan was sitting on a pedestal, surrounded by at least ten helpers. Morgan could not see Chindachchan's face. He could only see the raised arms.

After the Arayoda was in place, the volunteers and trustees threw a mix of turmeric and sandalwood into the burning embers, symbolising purification. To signal that the Theyyam was now ready to come to the Meleri, the drumbeats moved to a beautiful rhythm known as Theepanakkam.

The temple trustees opened the first donation box, tipped the money into a mundu, and brought it to Irumukhan. Chindachchan the Theyyam did not open the bundle but ordered that the money be given to Kelan. Kelan hobbled forward on one leg and bowed to Irumukhan in reverence.

'I have heard that these days you are too poor to even buy salt. The days of dire poverty are now over. Right, my friend?' Chindachchan took a break from the intense rituals to exchange pleasantries with Kelan.

In a symbolic act before the Theyyam jumped into the Meleri, the Oracle, the Komaran, grabbed the Theyyam's sword from his waist and ran towards the fire. As the audience watched the Oracle, Kangaani gave Giri a secret instruction. Giri took a dagger from his waistcoat and sliced at the rope that was meant to pull the Theyyam back from the fire. The rope weakened and was now held up only by a slender thread.

Giri then pretended to use the knife to adjust the stray palm leaves on the Theyyam's waist dress.

Cheers erupted from the crowd as Chindachchan, playing the Irumukhan Theyyam, walked towards the Meleri. He dived into the pile of burning wood with the ease of a child jumping playfully into a pool. The Theyyam bent his legs backwards in the air and crashed into the embers. Almost immediately, the attendants pulled him back. The attendants on standby helped the Theyyam get back to his feet. On the Meleri, a red-hot channel marked a path along which the Theyyam had been pulled back. The Theyyam took a few steps forward and again rushed into the pile of embers. Attendants scurried, using coconut boughs and brooms to sweep away stray cinders from the Meleri as the Theyyam was pulled away. They stood behind the Theyyam and circled the Meleri. One round of the performance was done.

Kaanaadi kept count until the twenty-third round. Then, everything went haywire. Giri's rope snapped and he fell backwards. Dasan, the puller who was on the opposite side, was stumped, but he hesitated only for a moment. He used all his strength and brought the Theyyam up to the ground.

The front-row audience rose from their seats, their screams at a fever pitch. Because the Theyyam had been pulled up with a single rope, embers flew all over the ground when he fell. Ignoring the smouldering pieces of fire on the floor, the attendants rushed in and brought the Theyyam up. Kaanaadi swallowed, not knowing what to do.

'The rope is broken. You must stop the Theyyam, Andhreessha ...' Kelu hobbled up to Kaatti in panic. But Kaatti was unmoved.

'Unless the Theyyam falls into the fire one hundred and one times, we cannot hold him back. That is the tradition,' he said with a tone of finality.

Kelu couldn't believe his ears. He heard the crowd's screams as the Theyyam dived into the fire one more time. Dasan, who had been looking expectantly at Kaatti to stop the proceedings, was unprepared for that move. As soon as the Theyyam hit the Meleri, the coiled rope in Dasan's hand came undone and he tumbled backwards. The rope slipped out of Dasan's hand and was hurled into the edge of the Meleri.

For a moment, the Theyyam lay face down on the embers, with no one to pull him upwards. There was no time to think. Sachin removed his second mundu from his upper body and jumped into the Meleri. He lost his balance when he bent down to pick up the rope. He tumbled down the heap of embers, but he succeeded in throwing the rope to the ground. With great difficulty, two attendants pulled the Theyyam away from the fire.

Kelan put his crutches away and fell at Kaatti's feet. 'You must stop the Theyyam, Andhreessha. He has embers inside his Arayoda. His legs are all burned.'

Nandanar shouted out from behind Kaatti. 'The Theyyam cannot be stopped over such minor challenges.'

'One more word out of you, and I will chop your head off!' The head of the Ettunaad army pointed a finger at Nandanar.

Even though his finger was pointed at Nandanar, Kaatti realised he was the target. Kelan begged and pleaded, but Kaatti stood firm.

The Theyyam jumped up and down, and then again headed to the Meleri. Dasan put one leg back, flung himself forward, and hit the Theyyam's waist dress with his head to stop him from diving into the fire again.

Without waiting for instructions, the Ettunaad army took matters into their hands. They created a human wall around the Meleri to stop the Theyyam.

Kaanaadi pushed and shoved people and slowly forced his way out of the crowd and went inside the temple. He found the Kshetrapalakan Theyyam sitting on a stool outside the inner chamber. With his head bowed and tears streaming down his face, Kaanaadi narrated what was happening outside.

The Kshetrapalakan put out his left hand to comfort Kaanaadi. His hands were adorned with ixora flowers and a tiger claw. Kaanaadi took his hand and helped him stand up. The boy who stood beside the Kshetrapalakan holding the aarti plate now walked ahead of them with a lighted brass lamp. The crowd split into two to let them pass. The eight elders rubbed their eyes in surprise. They were shocked to see Irumukhan's protector deity, who normally stayed within the temple, come up to the Meleri. The Kshetrapalakan shot them a fiery look.

The Kshetrapalakan Theyyam's right hand, the Ettunaad Army, bowed their heads to him. The Kshetrapalakan ordered that the Irumukhan Theyyam be stopped then and there.

'Aatmam … shall I?' Irumukhan sought permission, first from Kshetrapalakan and then from the audience, to stop. Everyone, including Morgan, nodded their heads in approval.

Achchan Namboodiri seemed flustered as he rushed to take charge of the situation. 'Just remove the headdress alone. One of you can come along and remove the rest of the costume on the way. He is fully burnt. We need to get him to the hospital. Quick! Come on, Kangaani.'

A Jeep came speeding along, brushing against the shoulders and arms of the people in its way. Dasan's hands flew as his dagger slashed the Theyyam's headdress off Chindachchan. Sachin, who had fainted by then, was carried into the Jeep. Giri and Raghavan jumped into the vehicle. Dasan pushed his way to the front of the crowd. He grabbed Sachin's outstretched leg and hauled himself into the rear of the Jeep, barely holding on.

Kelan hobbled his way to the Jeep, holding up the money Chindachchan had given him. 'Help him, my Lord! Use this money.' He laid the mundu with the offerings at Achchan Namboodiri's feet.

'I have enough money on me. Don't worry, Kelan. I will take care of him.' Achchan Namboodiri climbed into the vehicle and the Jeep fled away from the crowd like a wounded pig.

With each step, Kuttan wondered if he should go ahead or return home. He had seen the Thottam last night. The plan was to sleep for a couple of hours and then head back to the temple before dawn. But he fell into a deep slumber. It was daylight when he woke up with a start. He rushed out of home without glancing at the clock. He was regretting it now. He tried to guess the time by gauging the sun's intensity. The Theyyam would be over by now. Was there any point in going to the temple? He would have to walk back disappointed by this very route. He saw Dasan walk downhill towards him.

'Is the Theyyam over, Dasetta?' Kuttan asked.

Dasan didn't answer. He walked past Kuttan, his head bowed.

Kuttan stepped on a rock and, from the top of the Peelimudi, craned his neck to see if he could spot people returning after the Theyyam. When he saw Achchan Namboodiri's Jeep parked in the woods below, he decided he had to get to the Jeep.

A few days ago, he had stolen a few pieces of coloured chalk from the school and hidden them in a hollow under that Jeep. He had seen the Jeep parked under the gooseberry trees at the school, and thought it was the perfect hiding place. Rains were rare during the Theyyam season. So, he was sure the stolen chalk sticks would remain undamaged.

Kuttan held on to some wild creepers and carefully began his descent from the hilltop. He could hear Achchan Namboodiri's voice from a distance. So, he treaded softly as he got closer.

'You are sneering at me … probably because I am targeting you when you are totally vulnerable. There is a saying in Sanskrit. You may not have heard it. Horses and elephants are never offered as sacrifices. A tiger is never chosen. Only the goat is sacrificed in any ritual. Even God destroys the weak.'

Kuttan raised his head to see who Achchan Namboodiri was speaking to. A shiver ran down his spine.

Chindachchan was seated by the wheels of the Jeep in the full splendour of his Theyyam costume. Giri stood beside him, pinning Chindachchan's shoulders with an iron rod.

Namboodiri, with a wooden ladle, was hauling out blazing coals from an iron trunk and pouring them down

Chindachchan's chest, into his waist dress. Kuttan put his hands over his mouth to muffle his own scream. Instinct led him to slowly back away into the nearby thicket. Raghavan heard a sound and looked around. All he could see were swaying branches.

'The rope broke, and a few embers entered his garment. But why are none of the bones in his arm broken?'

It took a few seconds for Giri to grasp what Achchan Namboodiri was trying to say. He tightened his grip on the iron rod and bored into Chindachchan's shoulders with even greater force. He then moved the rod up to his throat.

Kuttan's eyes were tightly shut, but Chindachchan's final shrieks pierced his ears and tore into his soul.

The Lion Roars Again

Kelu Panikkar leisurely washed his hands and feet at the tap by his garden. He was gargling vigorously when he glanced around his yard. He saw a sight he couldn't look away from.

In the shadows of a banana tree, a man wearing a tiger mask stood staring at him. All the stories he had heard about the Lion flashed through Kelu's head. The Tiger raised his hand and beckoned him over.

Panikkar forgot to turn off the tap and followed the Tiger, as if in a trance. That walk in the dark ended in the middle of the rubber plantation next to his house. As Panikkar expected, the Lion was waiting for him. He was seated on top of a rock, like an emperor on his throne.

Kelu Panikkar spat out the words he had been rehearsing through the long walk. 'I have done no wrong. I haven't even hurt an ant. Then and now, I have only loved and respected Chindan. I had warned Giri many times. I told him not to accept the Kodiyila that rightfully belongs to Chindan's children. I haven't done anything that would bring infamy or disgrace to Chindan. I won't ever do that. Spare me! I have done no wrong.'

Against flashes of light from the rubber smokehouse and the shadows of the night, the vision of the Lion looked eerie.

'I am sorry for what is about to happen here. I truly am. So, I will give you a painless death.'

The Lion descended from the rock.

'I know you did no wrong. I need Giri. You are simply a pawn for me to get to him. Using small fish as bait to land larger fish does not mean the small fish has done something wrong. That is just the nature of hunting.'

The Tiger, sitting on a tall branch, threw a noose around Panikkar's head. As Panikkar gasped for air under the tree, the Lion soaked in the cool breeze on his return to Ekarmala.

'There is no hurry. The body will be brought for cremation only after Giri arrives tomorrow.' Ravi was at the crematorium, instructing the staff who were laying out coconut shells to build the pyre. He reversed his scooter in a hurry.

The flight landed at 3.40 a.m. Ravi and Raghavan travelled with the driver to pick up Giri from the airport. On the way home, Giri leaned back in his seat. He was silent. Ravi wasn't sure how to start a conversation, so he looked at the darkness outside the window.

Giri leaned forward and tapped the driver on his shoulder. 'If you are sleepy, Thambi can drive the car.'

The driver wasn't particularly tired, but he could not let go of an opportunity to rest. He stopped the car and went and sat in the rear seat. Raghavan had never met Thambi, the pale, middle-aged man who had travelled with Giri. Thambi battered the gear and the steering with all the grace of an amateur slaughtering an animal. Raghavan was too scared to go back to sleep.

Giri refused to speak to anyone, even after his father's funeral. He stayed cooped up upstairs, rarely stepping out and never meeting visitors.

Rumours flew about the man who had accompanied Giri. He was out of jail after killing a family of eight for gold. No, no … he was a hangman for the Arabs. He was a sorcerer whom Giri had brought in from Palakkad. Whenever Thambi took Giri's car out for a spin, people stopped to stare in admiration.

Raghavan tried to drop a hint when they met over drinks one evening. 'It is tiring to be stuck at home like this. People have been talking. They say we are too scared to go out in public.'

Giri sat on a cane chair, his hands clasped. 'Isn't there a meeting of the Ettunaad Council at the temple tomorrow? We will go there.'

Giri went to the meeting the next day with a large blue packet. 'Here's twenty lakhs. Consider it a small contribution from me.' He placed the packet on one of the steps.

Everyone present at the meeting was speechless. They looked at each other in wonder. Even Raghavan was stunned. Of course, he had guessed that Giri would throw money at the meeting. But he had thought the amount would be limited to a couple of lakhs.

'Many of you have already spoken about the serial murders going on here. My father was last in the line of those who were brutally killed. It is an open secret that everybody thinks I will be the next target. No one has said so openly, but I know it's on your mind. I have no reason to fear the killer because I have done no wrong. But the killer has been relentlessly harming people based on a mere misunderstanding. Verpuli Korachchan mentioned that the killer is Chindachchan's ghost—I am pretty sure no one on this council believes that. No rational man will believe this nonsense. Most of you know that it is Chindachchan's children, Aadi and Saravanan, who are carrying out these gruesome murders. You are only pretending to be unaware of this fact.'

He paused. 'If you don't believe me, I can prove it.'

The room was silent.

'I am going to be here for four more days. Lock up Aadidev and Saravanan until I leave inside this temple. If you keep them under supervision, I can guarantee you that a lot of lives, including mine, will be spared. You will also get the proof that they orchestrated all these murders.'

The idea of inconveniencing two young men was largely acceptable to the crowd. Seven of the village elders agreed with Giri. Verpuli Korachchan, however, raised his hand in dissent. Kaatti, the lamp-lighter, backed him up. Giri's suggestion was dismissed without much deliberation.

That night, Raghavan dug into a piece of fried chicken as he opened up to Giri. 'When the cops came, you shouldn't have told them that you don't have any suspicions about your father's death, Giri. Cops are smart these days. Had you mentioned Aadi's name, they would have hauled him away. One day with the cops, and he would have crumbled. No point raising this with the Ettunaad Council. Those hundred people have one hundred and ten opinions about the smallest of things. And you wasted so much money there for this ...'

'I know that. I tried to force my opinion on them. Then, the cops … What you said is true. If the cops get hold of these boys, they will peel their skin off. Peel, peel, peel. And finally, they will reach me. There will be an enquiry into Chindachchan's death. Forget all this. I have another plan. My words may have been wasted yesterday, but, from tomorrow, everyone will be on my side. For that, we need people to first turn against the murderers. These people consider the temple as the purest space. Slaughter a man and hang him up in the temple. That is all we need to rouse the public. They will sway our way. It's nothing new. Wherever ritual killings take place, people have been known to slay their enemies and blame it on the ritual.'

Giri was pecking at a bowl of cashew nuts. Raghavan filled a glass with liquor to take it to Thambi, who was slouched against the wall in a corner of the room.

'What people say is that we deliberately delayed getting Chindachchan to the hospital that day. So, one of the people who were in that Jeep along with Chindachchan needs to go. But then, only you and I from that group are still alive. So, why not bump off Kaatti? He is the Andhithiriyan. He did not know of our scheme. But when Chindachchan got injured that day, he was the one who insisted that the Theyyam jump into the fire again.' The minute he finished speaking, Raghavan knew he had said the wrong thing. The towel around his head came loose, and he shivered.

He heard Giri say, 'So, shall we do what Raghavan says, Thambi?'

The swish of a machete was the answer to that question. One strike and Raghavan spun like a top, blood gushing out from everywhere. Thambi made a few cuts above the waist, and then in a move he had mastered over time, slashed Raghavan's legs so that he fell flat on the ground.

'Not enough! Not enough!' Giri, with a drink in his hand and legs on the table, wasn't yet satisfied. Thambi moved forward with his weapon held tight.

Ettunaad woke up even before daybreak the next day. The committee members who had come to the temple for the pre-dawn fireworks ceremony first spotted the body hanging from the temple bell. Word spread and a sea of humanity descended on the temple grounds.

The Ettunaad Council called for an emergency meeting of the eight elders in a room behind the temple treasury building. Verpuli Korachchan hung his head in shame.

When the police came to investigate, Aadi's name did not come up. The Council had already warned the people gathered to keep mum. The police left, as usual, with no clues or list of suspects.

But the real policemen of Ettunaad soon came in search of Aadi and Saravanan. As the head of the Ettunaad Army, Sreejith informed them about the Council's decision. Aadi did not utter a single word in protest.

A large room was cleaned up for Aadi and Saravanan on the first floor of the treasury building. Aadi wasn't displeased. A stream of visitors flowed in until dusk. Some of them believed they were innocent. Some brought food.

Giri dropped in the next morning. 'Da … you are proving that foolishness runs in the blood of your family.' Aadi gave him a searing glance through the window bars. Giri tried to smile.

'I can slash your neck as easily as I kill a chicken. But that is not my way of doing things. It's not that I am not capable of strangulating you right here, right now. But strength should not be put down with strength. When fighting strength with strength, we face too many losses. Betrayal is the only weapon against strength. I will prove it to you in a few months, once I have left this place. My flight is at 7 p.m. on Wednesday. If I don't die by then, you can prove your fake innocence. If I leave as fit as I arrived, then you will be held responsible for all the murders that happened here. Consider yourself lucky if the villagers merely lynch you.' Giri looked Aadi straight in the eye. When he got no response, he tapped the window bars, smiled sarcastically, and went away. Aadi looked at their room. Saravanan was seated on the floor, his back against a wall. Sreejith was clipping his nails, pretending not to have heard what Giri had said.

After a while, Sreejith spoke up. 'What Giri says is true. If something dangerous happens to him while you are here, you can walk out of this room like a king. But if the reverse happens, you will have a lot of questions to answer.' He picked up the pieces of Saravanan's nails and put them in his pocket.

'If I am in here, all I can do is utter a few abuses against him. What else can I do?' Aadi gripped the window bars and looked down.

On the stairway, Kaatti strained against the wall to avoid contact with an unkempt young man coming up. The young man wore a shirt splattered with mud, and his hair was uncombed.

Once upstairs, Akhil, the young man, held out a pack of cigarettes through the window bars.

Aadi came to the window. He tore off the top of the pack. 'What's up?'

'Everything is set,' Akhil spoke in a low voice.

'Has Morgan come?'

Akhil pulled out a lighter and lit a cigarette for Aadi. 'Sir came this morning. He is with Kodumudi Annan in our shed in the quarry.'

'Kuttan?'

'He is downstairs, in the Jeep. If he comes up, people will notice.'

'Hmmm … Eda, nothing should go wrong. Leave no room for error.'

'I will take care of it.'

Akhil put his lighter away, shot a pointed glance at Aadi, and made his way back down.

As soon as he was out of sight, Sreejith remarked in a loud voice: 'Does he sleep with the wild hogs?'

'He's our boy, Sreethetta … He looks fierce but is a real softie.' Aadi threw the packet of cigarettes at Sreejith.

Giri was thrilled that he could once again fearlessly travel on his familiar routes after so many years. He got into a Jeep with Saamy.

'Saamietta, you took so much trouble to build this business and make it a success. Now, you're throwing it all away and leaving town. That upsets me … I don't understand this decision.'

'Think about yourself. However comfortable the Gulf is, won't you come back here after a certain age? You will come back to live in this godforsaken, primitive place, isn't that right?'

Giri found himself nodding in agreement.

Saamy, who was in the driver's seat, talked incessantly. 'A stone quarry means relentless profits. If you live close to the site, though, your business is hanging by a thread. One complaint and you are in trouble. And as you know, there is no shortage of pesky insects in your town. Our quarry is in the middle of a four-acre plot. So, I don't see any trouble for you in the future. You step out of the property and there are no homes for at least two to three kilometres. It is unlikely you will face complaints or cases. Put in some money and the profits are solid. I am not saying this because I am selling the quarry to you. Every day we send granite to Kozhikode. I have about thirty lorries on hire at any given point in time. The machines are all new. There is a shed where the workers live. I put up a post myself, so electricity is not a problem. I also have a JCB excavator and four Bharat Benz trucks. You, Giri, are the only person with the money and power to buy all this in one go. The best part of the deal is that the area yet to be excavated is about four times the land we have quarried so far. You will understand what I am talking about when we get there.'

Quarrying on your own land is a good idea, Giri thought. The sights outside were pretty. But the jerks and bumps on the road excavated by a backhoe were extremely uncomfortable.

Saamy stopped and put his hand out of the Jeep to stop a JCB approaching them.

'Eda … put that garland down and come drive this Jeep.'

He turned to Giri. 'This is our driver boy. Let him drive. I will sit on the other side. Could you scooch over a bit?'

Saamy got out of the driver's seat and walked to the other door of the Jeep. He sat next to Giri.

'Da … drive slowly. Don't jerk and lurch. I have a backache.'

Saamy spread out and made himself comfortable after the driver got in. Giri was squashed in the middle.

The driver shifted gears. 'Easy for you to say. But how do I take this jalopy ahead without a few jerks?'

Saamy put his arm around Giri's shoulder and looked at the driver. 'Don't blame the vehicle, da … This is an ancient Jeep. When your Aadi's father fell into the fire, this was the Jeep that took him to the hospital. Isn't that why your Aadiettan bought this vehicle after a long search?'

Saamy's words tore into Giri's ears. For a moment, he wondered if Saamy had uttered those words, or if he had imagined it. Giri looked around the Jeep anxiously. The Jeep was broken and rusty, certainly not a vehicle a rich man like Saamy would own.

Akhil, the driver, turned to Giri. 'Was he taken in this Jeep? No wonder he died! How could they have reached the hospital in time?'

'Aye … that wasn't the vehicle's fault. That's a long story. Speaking of stories … do you write books? Aadi mentioned something the other day,' Saamy asked Akhil.

Akhil kept his eyes fixed on the road. 'Aadiettan was only bluffing. Nothing like that.'

'A story worth a book will play out today. That's why I asked.'

Saamy turned to Giri. 'Listen, Giri! The quarry is in good shape. But there are many workers like this fellow who know nothing about the job. Quarrying requires skill. If a man like Akhil uses his JCB here, all you would get is useless stones contaminated by clay. Now that I think about it again, I don't suppose you can run this place with idiots like him. What if we cancel our deal? What do you think, Akhil?'

The driver laughed. 'Well, what's the point in giving all this to him? When he dies, will he take the stones and the quarry along with him?'

'Stop the car! I need to get out!' Giri raised his voice.

'Stop the car, da! Giri sir needs to get out.' Saamy made sure he was louder than Giri.

'Saamietta … don't talk nonsense. I am not your slave that I will start and stop the car whenever you command me to. This vehicle won't stop here. I know where it will stop.' Akhil shifted gears and drove faster.

Saamy tightened his grip on Giri's shoulder. 'When the boy speaks so sternly, what can we do, Giri?'

Giri held on as tightly as he could to the Jeep's iron bar and gritted his teeth. The Jeep climbed up a hillock and was back again on flat ground.

At the end of a lonely path strewn with Mysore Pipewort, the shadowy figures of two men emerged. Giri thought they could be waiting for them. The Jeep spluttered and gasped and took its time to reach the two men. The men were wearing tiger masks. Giri felt as if he was enveloped in darkness.

'Where are you headed, o Tigers?' Akhil asked them playfully.

'To the moon … Why are you so curious?'

Saamy signalled to the two men. 'There is a lot of space in the Jeep. We'll give you a ride.'

One of the Tigers was stout and short. The other was lean and shrivelled up. As soon as they got in, the Jeep resumed its journey. There was a mirror in front of Giri, but he was too afraid to look back at the men. The Jeep burrowed deeper into the quarry. It climbed up and down roads that seemed to have been laid in a hurry. Giri looked around with hope, but there was not a soul in sight. The Jeep went down a steep slope and landed on the ground where stones were cut. It turned left and stopped at a flatland surrounded by large anthills.

The Lion was seated on a makeshift throne made of bricks, with his back straight, one leg crossed over the other, and hands held together.

Saamy held Giri by the shoulder as they walked out. As they got closer, Giri dragged his feet.

The Lion rose to welcome Giri. 'Losses are high when you are in unfamiliar territory. I am not a skilled murderer as you may have heard. So, my lack of familiarity might cause you more pain.'

One of the two Tigers walked over to the Lion, swinging his iron rod. 'You are being unnecessarily courteous. From what I have seen and heard, you, indeed, are the King of the Kill. This murder too will be flawless.'

'Only fools are softened by flattery. But I am happy. May your tongue turn to gold,' the Lion raised his palm in a mock blessing.

The Lion's nails were adorned with claws. His hands gleamed an unnatural white.

The Tiger folded his hands in reverence towards the Lion. Giri wondered if he should do the same. But his hands no longer listened to him.

Saamy jumped onto the bonnet of the Jeep and put an arm around Akhil's shoulder. 'Have you seen those goods carriers that transport wood? Even if the truck overturns, the wood doesn't fall off. Do you know why?'

Akhil was glued to the drama playing out in front of him. 'My Saamietta, can't you ask your questions after this is over?'

'Tell me why… there's a reason I am asking you now.'

Akhil joined Saamy on the bonnet. 'That is because the wood is packed tight.'

'No. After the wood is securely tied, a stick is wedged into the knot and twisted at a right angle. This technique is called Mangalore Marikkal. Use this technique and even if the lorry turns turtle, the wood will remain intact.'

As Giri listened to Saamy's words, the Tigers were stretching out Giri's legs and tying fat iron rods to his limbs. They tightened the knot on the soles of his feet and fastened it with another small iron rod.

The Tigers asked Giri in a voice dripping with sarcasm. 'Do you have any last wishes left before you die?'

Giri's reply was swift. 'I … I want to see your face.'

The Lion roared like a beast and let out a loud laugh. He put his hands behind his head and removed the knots that held up his mask. The mask fell and the Lion's face came into view. One look at the face and Giri shut his eyes.

Crab motifs around the eyes. Swirls on side of the cheeks. A crescent moon on the forehead. Kozhi Pushpam, denoting the comb of the rooster, on both sides of the nose. There was one extra feature which was never found in the face of the Irumukhan Theyyam. The mouth seemed like the wide-open fangs of a lion, the ferocious teeth were glittering.

The Tigers and the Lion twisted and tightened the small iron rod at least five times to break Giri's legs. It wasn't a sight Saamy had the stomach to watch. He walked away long before they made the first twist. But even though he was far away, Giri's frantic screams as the life seeped out of him reverberated in his ears.

Along with the sight of Giri's body hung up on a tripod, one more curious vision greeted the onlookers in the temple yard. A vaar tree that had stood upright for ages had been uprooted, despite no strong winds. A part of the temple treasury had caved in when the top of the tree fell on the building.

The schoolteacher who doubled up as an astrologer came to visit. Ettillam Kannan Mooppar showed him the ruins of the treasury.

'A long time ago, during Chindachchan's time, the Theyyam proclaimed that the temple needed a new "Ghantaravam". What he meant was a new bell. Our people misheard that as "Bhandaaram", a storehouse for offerings and temple wealth,' the teacher laughed.

'Yes, yes. None so deaf as those who will not hear. They immediately started building this storehouse. In any case, our people only have eyes for money,' Kannan Mooppar said. His barb hit the teacher. A few days ago, Kaatti had gone to the teacher's house to formally request an astrological investigation at the temple. Kaatti had given him subtle directions on what the stars should reveal. In return, he had stealthily passed on a fat bundle of currency notes stained with the holy turmeric ash.

'The Kodiyila should be returned to Chindachchan's heirs. Chindachchan should be worshipped in the form of a Theyyam. Wood from the vaar tree that was felled should be used to build the new Theyyam's throne. A society where even the dead get justice is the only one that is truly alive. Kunki then. And now, Chindan the Lion.'

The teacher used cowrie shells and mantras to divine possible remedies for the recent catastrophes. A wave of applause greeted him when he announced his findings. In twenty-one days, the dates for the new Theyyam season were announced. The days flew by in a blink.

When Saravanan lay down before him to get his face painted, Sachin pinched himself to ensure he wasn't dreaming. The Purapuri temple was playing host to a crowd beyond its seating capacity. A delirious Aadi sat in the front row, pleased at the sight of the milling crowds. For a moment, he thought he saw George and Anand in the crowd. He shook his head and looked again. It wasn't them.

He was still searching the crowds when Morgan whispered in his ears that it was time for the Theyyam to set out. When the drumbeats changed to herald the Theyyam's arrival, Aadi forgot everything else.

Screams and shouts from the crowd drowned out the war cries from the Ettunaad Army.

And then, a hush. Aadi, Kaatti, the crowd, every grain of mud outside the temple—all waited breathlessly for the first steps of the Lion's dance.

Also from ekadā